DEAL WITH THE DEVIL

Jessie gritted her teeth and made up her mind, forcing herself to smile at Amador in what she hoped was a seductive manner.

"Colonel," she said in a throaty voice, "come here." She was aware of the sidelong look Ki had just given her but she did not acknowledge it. "I want to make a bargain with you."

"You who are about to die—what have you to bargain with, my pretty one?"

Jessie let her hands slide slowly down her body. Her eyes bored into Amador's but she did not speak—she did not have to.

Amador moaned, his eyes hungrily roving her form. "What do you want?" he asked huskily.

"I want you to spare Ki's life."

"In exchange for which you will—" Amador began, but Jessie interrupted him.

"Yes, I will," she whispered convincingly. . . .

Also in the LONE STAR series from Jove

WESLEY ELLIS

LONE STAR

AND THE
GEMSTONE ROBBERS

J

JOVE BOOKS, NEW YORK

LONE STAR AND THE GEMSTONE ROBBERS

A Jove Book / published by arrangement with the author

PRINTING HISTORY
Jove edition / February 1991

ISBN: 0-515-10513-9

Jove Books are published by The Berkley Publishing Group,
200 Madison Avenue, New York, New York 10016.
The name "JOVE" and the "J" logo
are trademarks belonging to Jove Publications, Inc.

PRINTED IN THE UNITED STATES OF AMERICA

10 9 8 7 6 5 4 3 2 1

LONE STAR

AND THE
GEMSTONE ROBBERS

Chapter 1

The town was crowded with people when the half-Japanese, half-American named Ki rode into it. Wagons and lone horsemen filled the streets, which had been turned into a muddy bog as a result of the early morning rain that had drenched the area.

People hurried in and out of shops, their arms filled with packages. Sounds filled the air: the loud pounding of iron on iron from the blacksmith's shop at the edge of town; the tinny twittering of a cuckoo clock coming from the interior of the jeweler's shop across the street; the thud of boots on the boardwalk; the giggle of a clutch of girls as they emerged from the milliner's shop a few doors away.

Ki watched the girls, a bevy of swaying hips and bouncing breasts, come toward him. He touched the brim of his flat-topped black Stetson and gave them all a sly smile. They flounced on by him, not daring in their pretended innocence to be so bold as to acknowledge the provocative salutation of a stranger. He shrugged and went inside the Mercantile.

"Hello, there, Ki," an aproned and sleeve-gartered man behind the store's counter called out. "Long time no see."

"How are you, Jed?"

1

"I'd be a whole helluva lot better, Ki, were I without these damned bunions of mine. They're killing me bit by slow little bit."

"Sorry to hear that."

"I soak 'em and I slice 'em with the missus's paring knife, but nothing does any good. They just keep on hurting and growing bigger by the minute. But never mind about my woes. What can I do for you today?"

Ki thrust a hand into a pocket of his jeans and came up with a folded sheet of paper. "Ed Wright, when he heard I was coming into town today, asked me to give you this."

Jed took the piece of paper from Ki and unfolded it. Putting on a pair of spectacles and raising his eyebrows, he peered at it. "How is Miss Starbuck's ranch foreman these days?"

"Ed's fit as a fiddle."

"I envy him. Did I tell you about my bunions?" Jed lowered his head and peered at Ki over the rims of his spectacles. "Of course I did. I'm turning forgetful. Will you be taking the supplies on Ed's list back with you, Ki?"

"No, I won't. Ed said he'd send somebody in with a wagon to fetch them out to the ranch tomorrow."

"I'll have everything ready by then."

"Good day to you, Jed."

As Ki headed for the door, Jed called out, "Have you seen today's *Clarion Call*?"

"No," Ki replied, turning at the door and giving Jed an inquiring glance.

"There's a matter reported in the *Call*'s pages that might be of interest to you."

Ki left the Mercantile and stepped out onto the boardwalk. Now what was Jed getting at in his reference to the town's daily newspaper? Well, there was one sure way to find out. He headed across the street, dodging a spring wagon that came careening around a corner, and went into the

2

sundries shop that faced the Mercantile.

The odor of perfume was heavy in the air of the shop. Ki passed counters piled high with wooden toys, yarns and knitting needles, lace doilies, and the like and stopped in front of a magazine rack. He was about to reach for a copy of the *Clarion Call* when the lurid cover of the *Police Gazette* caught his eye.

His reaching hand halted in midair as he stared at the woman with the bright blond hair and terrified eyes displayed prominently on the *Gazette*'s front cover. She was struggling with a bearded man—a villain to be sure, judging by the evil glint in his badly bloodshot eyes—as he laid hairy hands upon her and her bodice ripped . . . .

Ki gazed longingly at the woman's plump breasts, which were about to escape from the red satin dressing gown she wore. He picked up a copy of the magazine and leafed through its bloody pages, which contained stories of rape and robbery, pillage and prostitution.

Prostitution.

He thought of Millie and the reason for his visit to town on this beautiful summer afternoon. Millie of the red hair and lithe body. Millie who knew more ways to please a man than Methuselah had lives.

He leafed through the *Gazette*.

" . . . the man's big gun spoke and the policeman fell, a round red hole appearing in the center of his forehead from which copious amounts of blood flowed . . . ."

Ki turned the page he had been reading, looking for the cover story. He couldn't find it. He shut the *Gazette*, replaced it on the rack, gave the woman on the cover one last longing look and picked up a copy of the current issue of the *Clarion Call*.

The newspaper was only four pages long, but the type was small, so a great deal of news was covered. Ki's eyes roved over the news of deaths and births, statewide political scandals, the need for contributions to provide the local

3

school with new sets of McGuffay's Readers. . . .

And then—there it was. On page four, under the heading "A Gala Event":

Ki, a gentleman known to one and all in our fair town and who is the close friend of one of the pillars of Texas society, Miss Jessica Starbuck, is to be feted at a party on Tuesday night.

The gala event, to be held at the renowned Starbuck Ranch, is being held to celebrate Ki's birthday. When your roving reporter questioned the lovely Miss Starbuck concerning her guest of honor's age, she coyly refused to reveal it. But Miss Starbuck was not loath to tell yours truly that there would be a four-piece orchestra present at the party to entertain invited guests. In addition, there will be an assortment of fine French wines sure to please the most discriminating palate and Cornish hens stuffed with a chestnut dressing and garnished with orange slices.

Miss Starbuck mentioned that, since this party is a very special occasion, she plans to wear the Starbuck Firebird which she graciously allowed this reporter to see. It is a truly impressive—nay, magnificent—brooch made from a large many-faceted and flawless ruby (hence its interesting name).

Miss Starbuck said the brooch has been in her family for many generations and as such is a highly prized heirloom. The Firebird belonged most recently to the late lamented Mrs. Sarah Starbuck, Miss Starbuck's mother and wife of entrepreneur Alex Starbuck. It is now the property of Miss Starbuck herself, who said of it, "Its monetary value is exceeded only by its great sentimental value for the Starbuck women who have, in their respective times, owned it."

Ki himself (alas!) was not present when your roving reporter called at the well-appointed home of Miss

Starbuck, so he could not be interviewed for this piece but . . .

Ki quickly scanned the remainder of the article. ". . . there will be dancing . . . Miss Starbuck told us that she and Ki have been friends for a good many years and have been through thick and thin together . . ."

Ki returned the newspaper to the rack and left the store, thinking that he had better be about his business if he was to complete it in time to return to the ranch before the party was to begin. He started down the boardwalk, taking long strides, and turned left at the intersection of Main and Poplar Streets.

Ki was taller than most men. He topped six feet and moved with a kind of feline grace. His body was lean but heavily muscled as a result of his years of martial arts training in more than one *dojo,* or practice hall, in Japan, where he had spent the early days of his youth. He wore his blue-black hair long; it hid his ears and the nape of his neck. His eyes were the color of almonds, their slight slant the only distinctly Oriental characteristic of his otherwise predominantly Caucasian features. The skin of his face was tawny and smooth except for the faint trace of lines at the corners of his eyes and mouth. Son of a Japanese mother and an American father, Ki had been in the employ of Alex Starbuck for years before the latter's death, and now he remained the close companion and friend of the deceased tycoon's daughter, Jessie.

He passed several houses and then stopped in front of a three-story brick building that had lace curtains in its many windows and a trainman's red lantern hanging beside the front door. He mounted the steps to the porch and knocked at the door. He stood there, trying not to fidget despite his eagerness to see Millie again. Then the door was opened by a portly woman wearing dangling emerald earrings and rings on nearly every pudgy finger of her hands.

5

"Ki!" she exclaimed, breaking into a smile, the ample flesh of her face almost extinguishing her eyes as she did so. "It's good to see you, as always. Come in, come in!"

"How've you been, Mrs. Murchison?" Ki asked as he was ushered into the huge parlor of the house.

"Can't complain. Yourself?"

"Fine, thanks. Is Millie here?"

"She's here. Let me give her a call." Mrs. Murchison went to the bottom of the stairs in the hall outside the parlor and called, "Millie! I've got a surprise for you, dear one. Come on down and see what—who—it is!"

"Be right there," a sultry female voice responded.

Mrs. Murchison returned to the parlor. "Drink, Ki?"

He shook his head. "It might interfere with my performance." His grin matched the one that spread across Mrs. Murchison's face.

"Have a bonbon then," she said, lifting the delicate lid of a porcelain candy box that rested on a table, revealing colorful candies inside.

Ki, more out of politeness than because he wanted one, chose a green candy. He was chewing it when a young woman came down the stairs and into the parlor. He almost swallowed the candy whole at the sight of her.

She was wearing a lavender dress that barely covered her pelvis and didn't cover most of the mounds of her large breasts. She wore slippers with white pom-poms on them and nothing else.

There was a beauty mark painted on her right cheek, and her lips and cheeks had been roughed. Her skin was pale as a result of the face powder she had delicately applied. An altogether desirable woman.

She put a hand to her short red hair and fluffed it as she stood there with her other hand resting on a hip she had thrust sideways. She smiled sweetly at Ki. "I thought you'd gone and forgotten all about me," she purred, her lips barely

6

parted to allow the words to escape. "You haven't been here in ages."

Ki went to her and took both of her hands in his. "I was here just last week—Friday it was."

"Well, it *seems* like ages since I've seen you," she declared. She began to back up, drawing Ki toward the staircase that led to the upper stories of the house.

As they climbed the stairs to the third floor, Ki idly wondered if the height they had reached was the reason he was feeling giddy. But no. He knew it was Milly, the provocative nearness and the exciting scent of her, that was unsettling him.

Once inside her room, she slipped her dress over her head and kicked her slippers across the room. She held out both hands. Ki went to her and they embraced.

"What's it to be this time, you sweet thing?" she whispered. Her words, which had just entered Ki's ear, were quickly followed by her hot tongue.

He told her what he wanted and then let her help him undress, a process Millie managed to make highly erotic. No fumbling on her part; every move she made was sure and certain. Ki trembled as her hands touched him here, there, everywhere. He felt himself stiffening, and then, as he dropped his jeans, his shaft snapped up to aim straight at Millie, who took it in one soft hand and began to gently stroke it.

She looked at him, winked and said, "It's time for me to get down to business."

To Ki's sensual delight, that is exactly what she did. She dropped to her knees in front of him and gripped his erection in one hot hand, studying it with a critical eye. Then she eagerly tasted it, her lips nibbling it, her tongue tickling it.

Ki put his hands, palms down, behind him on the bed and leaned back, prepared to enjoy her ministrations. Enjoy them he did as Millie's head bobbed up and down on his

7

stone-stiff erection and her tongue laved it. He exulted in the satin-soft embrace of her lips and reveled in the fiery furnace of her mouth. He could feel a spasm shoot through his testicles; he could sense the explosion that was coming.

Millie released him. "Let me catch my breath," she murmured, wiping her lips with the back of her hand.

Ki groaned his disappointment at her sudden withdrawal, but his groan faded away as she once again took him into her mouth and began to suck with a passion and intensity the likes of which he could not recall ever having experienced before. He shifted position slightly and thrust himself deeper into her mouth.

She gagged and started to withdraw, but Ki clasped his hands behind her head and held her in place, unwilling to let her go this time and thus lose the wild sensations she was stirring within him.

She was breathing heavily now and making wet sounds as he rose from the bed and stood before her, both of them locked together in an erotic embrace.

His hands remained clasped behind her head as she adjusted her own body to his new stance and began again to bob her head back and forth as she sucked his shaft. He began to move his hips. Soon he was matching her rhythm. As her head moved back, so did his pelvis. As her head moved forward, and her lips devoured inch after glistening inch of his shaft, so did his pelvis, so that his rigid lance of flesh disappeared completely into her mouth and her lips were momentarily pressed against the curly public hair darkening his crotch.

They kept at it for another minute and then it began. Ki could feel himself tightening, could feel himself getting ready to erupt. He braced himself, threw back his head, arched his neck, let out a cry of pure ecstasy—and the dam of his passion burst, flooding the kneeling Millie's mouth and throat.

She hungrily devoured his seed, firmly gripping his bare

thighs in both hands as she did so, her lips still encircling his rod. She kept at it until his hips stopped bucking and his hands fell away from the back of her head.

As he eased himself out of her mouth and sat down on the bed, she swallowed several times, bent forward, and began to lick his testicles.

He fell back on the bed, threw his arms out at his sides, closed his eyes, and gloried in what she was doing to him. Time no longer existed for him. Only Millie's tongue existed. Her tongue and his testicles. Her giving and his taking. He was lost in a world that had become one hot erotic delight, in a lusty sea in which he was happy to let himself drown.

Millie suddenly raised her head and cried, "Oh, golly, I almost forgot!"

Ki propped himself up on his elbows and stared at her. "Almost forgot what?"

"I read the paper this morning—the *Clarion Call*."

Ki wondered what she was talking about.

"Happy birthday!" Millie crowed and jumped on him, pushing him back down on the bed. She kissed him several times in quick succession. "I read all about the birthday party your girlfriend is giving for you tonight."

When Ki finally managed to get out from under Millie, he said, "Jessie Starbuck is not my girlfriend."

"Try telling that to His Holiness, the Pope," Millie taunted, wagging a playful finger in Ki's face. "He'd excommunicate you for sinful speaking."

Ki didn't argue. This was not the first time that someone had misinterpreted the nature of his relationship with Jessie, and he strongly suspected it would not be the last.

"I'm jealous," Millie announced, pretending to pout. "When you were here last Friday you swore you would remain totally devoted to me."

"Honey, I am totally devoted to you. Didn't I ask for you today when I could have asked for any one of the other girls who work for Mrs. Murchison?"

"Well—"

Ki planted a kiss on the tip of Millie's upturned nose.

"I guess I'll forgive you this time," she cooed. "But if I should happen to see you on the street with that woman, and you know what woman I'm talking about, I'll claw her eyes out. Yours too."

Ki began to dress. As he did so, Millie perched cross-legged on the edge of the bed. When he was finished dressing, he took some folding money from his pocket and peeled off a two-dollar bill, which he handed to Millie.

Shaking her head, she refused to take it from him.

"Is there something wrong with my money?"

"Today there is, yes."

"You never refused payment for services rendered before."

"Well, today is different."

"Different?"

"You mean you really don't know what I'm talking about?"

A perplexed Ki shook his head.

"Today's your *birthday*!" Millie exclaimed. "What I just gave you—consider it your birthday present."

"Millie—"

She reached out, took the two-dollar bill from Ki and stuffed it back into his pocket.

He bent down and kissed her full on the lips. Her arms encircled his neck. Their kiss lasted a good minute. Then he disengaged himself from her and said, "I thank you kindly for the birthday present. It was without the shadow of a doubt the best one I've ever gotten in my life."

Millie giggled and waved him out of the room.

Ki smiled at the pleasant memories of his afternoon encounter with Millie at Mrs. Murchison's parlor house as he rode across a stretch of tableland that was thick with grama grass.

10

The woman was a wonder. In more ways than one. Only Millie would have thought of giving a man a free blow job for a birthday present. He decided to match her thoughtfulness the next time he called on her. He would buy her the hat she had pointed out to him in the milliner's shop last Friday as they strolled together through the town, under the watchful eyes of the townsmen and the wagging tongues of their women. The hat with the ostrich plume encircling its wide crown.

He left the tableland and rode through a stretch of rolling hummocks that were covered with a thick growth of mixed sage and rabbitbrush. His horse shied when it spotted a sidewinder gliding through the dense ground cover, but it didn't bolt, thanks in large part to Ki's firm hands on the reins.

They were moving through a grove of cottonwoods in full green leaf when Ki saw the figure of a man up ahead of him. A man on foot. Now why, he asked himself as he studied the distant figure, would a man be way out here in the middle of nothing and nowhere without a horse to get him to where he wants to go? As he watched suspiciously, the figure swayed, staggered and fell to the ground.

He dug his heels into his horse and rode forward at a gallop until he reached the man. Then he dismounted and, kneeling beside the prone figure, gently turned him over. When he saw the face of the man, he winced. For two reasons. Because of the bloody gash in the man's left temple, through which could be seen blue-white bone, and because he recognized the injured man as an employee of Jessie's named Carl Landsman.

Landsman's eyes opened but not all the way. He stared blearily up at Ki for a moment and then raised his trembling hands to shield his bloodied head and cried in a cracked voice, "Don't! Don't hit me again!"

Ki gripped Landsman's shoulder with one hand. "Carl, it's me. Ki."

Landsman slowly lowered his hands. His eyes tried to

11

focus. He blinked. And then, "Ki?"

"Yes. What happened to you?"

Landsman tried to sit up but was unable to do so unaided. Ki helped him up into a sitting position. Landsman groaned and lowered his head.

"Who did this to you, Carl?"

"Two men. They were riding my backtrail for a while. They caught up with me. They rode along with me for a while. Seemed friendly enough fellows. We talked about this and that. But then, when we got to Deep Gulch, they showed their true colors. They threw down on me."

"Why?"

"I was driving twenty head of horses out to where our Abilene-bound herd's been bedded down for the last day or two. The boys needed fresh mounts for the drive north. I was going to turn the twenty head of stock I'd brought over to them and drive the remuda they already had back to the ranch. Those two jaspers that joined me, they wanted those horses and, by God, they got 'em, damn their eyes!"

"How'd that happen?" Ki pointed to the ugly wound on Landsman's temple.

"One of the bastards made me get down off my horse, and when I did he pistol-whipped me. By the time he was through with me, I was lost to the world, I can tell you. When I came to myself again, all the horses was gone, including my own, not to mention the two thieves who took 'em."

"Two against one," Ki mused. "Two armed men against one unarmed man."

"It sure wasn't a fair fight, that's for sure." Landsman gingerly touched his temple and groaned. "I can't feel a thing all around where they like to have split my skull wide open. Reckon they cut the nerves to ribbons on my forehead."

"I'll take you into town so the doctor there can sew you up. Can you ride?"

"I can ride, but I don't want no doctor. Not right now, I don't. What I do want is to get my paws on the son of a bitch who pistol-whipped me."

"You need doctoring, Carl."

"All in good time. Now that you're here, Ki, maybe you and me could go get those two—and Miss Starbuck's horses."

"That's what I was planning to do. But by myself. You—"

"I'm damn well going with you." Landsman got unsteadily to his feet and stood there for a moment before gaining his bearings.

"I really do think I ought to take you to town, Carl, and—"

"Enough talk and enough time wasting, Ki. I mean no offense, but let's be about our business. Those men have a good head start on us, though I reckon we can catch up with them if we hustle."

"Which way did they go?" Ki asked as he stepped into the saddle.

"That way," Landsman answered, pointing.

Ki put out a hand and helped Landsman climb up behind him.

Then the two men moved out, heading north after the horse thieves, one of whom had turned Landsman's forehead into a bloody ruin.

Ki followed the clear sign the horse herd had left as the thieves drove it across sandy ground, through brush and then across a vast expanse of rocky ground. He heard his quarry before he saw it. The pounding of hooves up ahead was a sullen thunder. As his horse crested a low ridge, Ki saw the herd and the two men flanking it.

"That's them," Landsman said from behind him. "The one on the left—the one with the walleye—he's the one practiced his skull-busting skills on me."

"They're heading for Eagle Canyon," Ki observed. He wheeled and then heeled his horse. "Come on."

13

"Where the hell are we going?" a startled Landsman asked as they rode back down the ridge they had just crested.

"We're going to circle around," Ki told him. "We'll ride over that way, round the ridge, and if we're fast enough and lucky enough, we'll be at the far end of Eagle Canyon waiting for those fellows when they come riding out."

"Let's go!" Landsman whooped, his voice gleeful.

They rode hard, Ki whipping his mount with the reins to force from it every bit of strength and speed it had to give. The horse didn't let its master down. It got them to the mouth of Eagle Canyon several important minutes before the horse herd reached it. Both men took advantage of those precious few minutes to plan their mode of attack. By the time the twenty Starbuck horses—their manes and tails flying and strings of saliva whipping from their parted lips as they galloped along under the goading of the two riders flanking them—appeared around a bend in the canyon, Ki and Landsman were ready for them.

Ki had dismounted and broken off a sturdy branch from a sycamore sapling by jumping up, gripping it in both hands and letting his weight snap it free of the tree's trunk.

Landsman was now in the saddle of Ki's horse, both hands on the reins, ready and obviously eager to make his move. He made it when the leader of the herd, a dapple, was no more than thirty feet from the mouth of the canyon. Spurring Ki's horse, Landsman headed toward the dapple at a sharp angle.

The horse, its wide eyes wild, saw him coming and swerved to the right to avoid a collision, which was exactly what Landsman and Ki had known it would do. The horses behind it also veered sharply, following their leader, as they all emerged from the canyon onto the open plain again.

Landsman continued bearing down on the dapple for a few minutes. Then, dropping back a bit, he aimed Ki's mount at the middle of the mass of tightly packed bodies. The herd, many of its members nickering nervously in alarm at this strange and totally unexpected development—a wild man aboard a horse bearing down on them—widened the angle of their flight.

In doing so, they collided with the walleyed man riding on their right flank, who was trailing a saddled and bridled horse. His horse went down hard, throwing him to the ground. The man scrambled along the ground on his hands and knees in a desperate attempt to get out of the way of the dozens of iron-shod horses pounding toward him.

He made good his escape—but just barely. One of the horses at the very rear of the herd leaped over him, its hooves almost striking his vulnerable back and buttocks. His horse and the one he had been leading went racing away and then stopped to look back over their shoulders at the galloping herd.

At the moment that Landsman had forced the horse herd to alter its course and head to the right, Ki went sprinting toward the animals. But they were not the object of his run. The mounted man on the herd's left flank was. The rider, surprised and angered at what Landsman had done and was still doing to stampede the herd in the wrong direction, was yelling and cursing at the top of his voice as he turned his own horse and went riding in pursuit of the stolen horses, which were widening the distance between him and them.

Thus, he did not see Ki coming toward him. But he felt the jarring impact of the tree limb that Ki wielded as it struck him across the back just above his gunbelt. He lost both his grip on the reins and his balance in the saddle and went toppling to the ground as his horse ran on.

Ki ran up to him as the man leaped to his feet and turned to face him, an angry gleam in his eyes.

"Drop your gunbelt!" Ki ordered, the tree limb in his hands held parallel to the ground, at the level of his chest.

"Drop my . . . ?" The man stared at Ki in disbelief. "You're telling me to drop my gunbelt and you're without a gun of your own to back up your bad-assed order?" The man began to laugh, a deep-throated booming sound that blended with the diminishing sound of the fleeing horse herd. Then he drew his gun in one lightning-swift move and cocked its hammer.

Ki shifted his grip on the tree limb, which he intended to use as a makeshift *bo*, an ancient weapon whose origins had been lost in the dim halls of time. The limb in Ki's hand was the form the *bo* probably had taken when it was first used by ancient Oriental warriors. Only later, over the centuries, did the *bo* become the "straight staff" used in modern martial arts combat.

Ki swung his *bo* outward and downward. It struck the gunman's wrist, causing his weapon to fall from his hand. He let out a strangled cry, grasped his right wrist with his left hand and did a little dance to try to control the pain he was feeling.

Ki moved in and was reaching for the gun on the ground when the man he had struck let go of his wrist and lunged, both hands wildly reaching for Ki.

Ki, again gripping the *bo* in both hands, used a *morote-uke*, a classic block, to prevent the man's hands from touching him. Then he thrust the *bo* forward, striking the man across the chest with his weapon and sending him stumbling backward.

The man quickly recovered his balance and lunged—this time not for Ki but for the gun he had dropped, which still lay on the ground some distance away from him.

Ki, stepping to the left, his knees bent, brought the left section of the *bo* down and then thrust the right section forward and up in a deft *naname-uchi*, a diagonal side strike, which caught his opponent full in the face and split his upper lip, from which a red jet of blood spurted.

Before the man could recover from the devastating blow, Ki, his legs firmly planted far apart and his knees bent to help him maintain his balance so that he would be able to use the *bo* most effectively, was about to deliver another blow, one he hoped would be the coup de grace, when the cursing man managed to seize the *bo* with both of his strong hands.

To counter the sudden if somewhat clumsy attack, Ki lunged toward the man, raised the right section of the *bo* high into the air with his opponent still holding onto it—and then brought the *bo*'s raised right section down in a wide arc. It struck the man on the left side of the face. His left hand lost its grip on the *bo* and fell away as his knees began to buckle.

Pressing his advantage, Ki thrust hard with his right hand on the still-descending *bo*, and the man went down on his back, his right hand falling free of the *bo*.

Ki, standing erect, following through on the movement that had brought the right section of the *bo* into contact with his enemy, raised the weapon so that one of its ends pointed downward at the horse thief lying on the ground. He raised it in preparation for a kill . . .

He couldn't do it. Didn't need to do it. His enemy had been utterly vanquished. He lay there, his eyes terror-filled, his hands helplessly raised as he tried to ward off the blow he saw coming, his bloody upper lip quivering.

Ki brought the *bo* down—slowly—until it touched the man's throat, effectively pinning him to the ground.

"That did it for the damned devil!" Landsman crowed delightedly, the gun he had taken from the walleyed man trained on his prisoner.

Ki looked up to see Landsman marching toward him, an incongruous smile on his still-bloody face.

"Drive that piece of tree right through his gullet while you're at it, Ki!"

But Ki didn't. Instead, he moved swiftly to where his downed opponent's gun lay. He picked it up, dropped the *bo* and ordered the man who had tried to kill him to get up.

The man did and stood shamefacedly before Ki, his arms

17

hanging at his sides, his eyes downcast.

"Looks like we each got our share of the miscreants," Landsman exulted, waving the gun in his hand at its former owner, who stood rigidly in front of him with his hands reaching for the clouds. "What's more, I got my mount back. This jasper was trailing it."

"What about the other horses?"

"They'll stop running now that there's nobody driving them. They should be easy enough to round up."

"We've got to do something about these two." Ki indicated his and Landsman's prisoners.

"I've got an idea. Let's see does it suit you, Ki. I'll take these two into town and hand them over to the marshal. Then I'll go see Doc Smithers and get my head patched up before my brains start spilling out on me. I will, that is, if you'll do me a real big favor and round up the herd and drive them out to where the boys are camped and waiting for them. Would you mind doing that for me, Ki?"

"Consider it done, Carl."

Landsman's smile evaporated. "Get on your horse, both of you," he barked at the cowed horse thieves. "We've got us some traveling to do."

As the silent and crestfallen pair of thieves complied with Landsman's order, Ki handed him the gun that had belonged to the man he had conquered.

He stood there and watched as Landsman, in the saddle of his horse, which the walleyed man had been trailing earlier, moved his two prisoners out, guiding his horse with knee pressure while he ignored the reins and trained both guns on the backs of the beaten horse thieves.

"So long, Ki!" he called back over his shoulder. "Thanks for your help. We make a helluva pair, don't we? Next time we ought to do even better since practice makes perfect, or so folks are fond of saying."

Ki, grinning, stepped into the saddle and rode out to

search for the horse herd, hoping he would be able to find and deliver them fast, since the sun was descending the sky and his birthday party, which was to be held at the Starbuck ranch, was due to begin at dark.

Chapter 2

"Where is Ki?" Jessie Starbuck asked as she placed beeswax tapers in a silver candelabra that rested in the center of the long buffet table set up in the middle of her ranch's great room. "He should have been back by now. Has anyone seen him?" she asked the maid and butler bustling about the room as they prepared things for Ki's birthday party.

"I have not seen Señor Ki," the white-coated and red-sashed Carlos answered as he placed a bottle of Madeira on the table next to dozens of sparkling crystal glasses.

"Nor have I seen him," echoed Esmeralda, who wore a stiffly starched white apron over her long black dress. "Will you have the orchestra by the window, señorita, or shall they play seated over there?" She pointed to the area next to the fireplace, above which hung a portrait of Jessie's deceased mother wearing a green gown.

"The windows, I think" Jessie responded, a finger on her chin as she surveyed the room. Then, "Oh, shooo!" She waved both hands to send several fuzzy bee flies winging away from the wild pink roses that stood in a porcelain vase on a table near the windows. "Shooo!" she repeated as the bee flies circled the room and returned to poke their long proboscises inside the rose blossoms, to suck nectar from them.

She went to an open window and waved the bee flies through it. She stood there at the window, her hands clasped in front of her, and stared at the horizon, below which the sun had slipped, leaving a crimson sky behind it and a land inhabited by purple shadows that were slowly turning black.

"If Ki misses his own birthday party—"

"He would not do that," Esmeralda said with a smile as she fluffed up pillows on a horsehair sofa. "He tells me himself only this morning that he would not miss the chance to have some of my *puchero*. He called it my 'famous *puchero*.'" Esmeralda blushed. "He always teases Esmeralda."

"Ki wasn't teasing," Jessie declared. "I can say that with confidence. I happen to know he adores your beef and veal stew. He once told me he had never tasted better. He said he could eat it every single day and twice on Sundays, it was that good. I'm happy to say I agree with his judgment."

"Gracias, señorita," said a beaming Esmeralda. "Do not worry. Señor Ki will come. If he is not here by the time I am to put out the *puchero*, *then* he will come for sure. You will see."

Jessie left the window as the sky turned from crimson to the color of old gold. "Carlos, you have someone ready to see to our guests' carriages this evening?"

"My son, Carlito, sí, Miss Starbuck. He is very excited about tonight. He wears, like me, the white coat and red sash. He thinks he looks quite magnificent."

"I'm sure he does." Jessie crossed the room to inspect the gleaming silverware fanned out on the buffet table and then the crisp white linen napkins marked with a scarlet letter S. When she was satisfied that everything was in order in the good and capable hands of Esmeralda and Carlos, she left the room and climbed the stairs to the second floor, where, in her tastefully furnished bedroom, she found the bath Esmeralda had prepared waiting for her.

She hurriedly removed her clothes and stepped into the

21

tub, wincing slightly as the hot water shocked her skin. She reached for some amber pins resting on her dressing table and used several of them to pin up her hair. As she did so, she caught a glimpse of herself in the full-length mirror attached to her closet door.

It showed her a tall lithe woman of exquisite proportions. A woman with long lean legs and delicately formed but strong arms and hands. She watched the woman in the mirror gently touch her pert breasts and then run her fingers down the curve of her waist and across the flat plain of her belly. The woman in the mirror had eyes the color of emeralds, which contrasted nicely with her lustrous hair that, depending upon the light, looked coppery or russet. She wore it long, and it seemed to attract light to it as a magnet attracts iron. Now it shimmered in the last fading rays of the day's dying sun.

With a sigh, she settled into the tub and began to rub her body and face with a soap scented by cloves. It was pleasantly smooth, against her equally smooth skin, and relaxing. She raised one leg out of the hot water and ran the bar of soap along its slender length until it was coated with a sudsy froth. Then she repeated the process with the other leg. Minutes later, she stood up, dripping soap suds and water, and began to towel herself dry. She stepped out of the tub onto a plush bath mat and bent over to dry her lower extremities, her rounded buttocks prominently displayed to no one. Once altogether dry, she slipped on a white silk robe and sat down in front of her dressing table mirror, where she unpinned her hair and, tilting her head first to one side and then to the other, began to brush it vigorously.

She had almost reached the self-imposed hundredth stroke when a light knock sounded on her bedroom door followed by the entry into the room of Esmeralda.

"He is come, Señor Ki," she announced with a bright smile. "He says to tell you he is sorry to be so late in coming but he could not help himself. Are you ready to dress, señorita?"

Jessie's hundredth stroke coincided with Esmeralda's question, which she answered with a nod.

Esmeralda, as Jessie rose and slipped out of her dressing gown, helped Jessie into her chemise and corset. The latter she laced tightly until Jessie let out a melodramatic groan as the corset's stiff stays pressed against her soft flesh. But Esmeralda's efforts, Jessie saw with satisfaction in her mirror, had managed to reduce the circumference of her waist to mere inches.

"Have you in mind the gown you will wear tonight, señorita?" Esmeralda inquired as Jessie put on her muslin petticoat and fluffed it out around her legs.

"Yes, my pink and green gown," she answered.

As Esmeralda went to the closet, Jessie donned her stockings and then her shoes. She was just finishing buttoning her white shoes when Esmeralda returned with the chosen gown, and Jessie slipped it on.

Esmeralda clasped her hands together and murmured, "So beautiful."

The gown had a cuirass bodice with a square-cut decolletage. It was moulded to the hips, ending in a V-shape in front, decorated with silk cord tassels in pink, and had green buttons. Its sleeves reached Jessie's elbows and ended in ruffles.

Jessie seated herself in front of her dressing table's mirror and, with the help of Esmeralda, parted her hair in the center and brushed the sides back into a chignon that exposed her delicate ears.

Then she opened her velvet-covered jewelry box and removed its top tray, which held a colorful assortment of jewelry. Below the tray, in a small, pink satin-lined nest, lay the ruby brooch she intended to wear that night, the heirloom that had come to be known in her family as the Starbuck Firebird.

23

Its many facets sparkled in the light. The large ruby had an oval shape and was the color of blood.

Esmeralda watched as Jessie pinned the brooch to her gown at the very center of her decolletage, where it glowed brilliantly.

Both women stared into the mirror at the jewel for a long moment before Jessie finally rose and, picking up a pair of pale pink gloves, slipped them on. Then, followed by Esmeralda, she left the bedroom and made her way downstairs.

Upon her arrival in the great room, she found the orchestra setting up and the first guests, Mr. and Mrs. Stanley Birkenhall, standing alone in the center of the large room.

"Stan," Jessie said and then, "Elizabeth." She went to them, embraced Elizabeth Birkenhall and gave her cheek to Stanley Birkenhall to be kissed.

"We're frightfully early, Jessie," Elizabeth said apologetically. "But I was in ever so much of a hurry to get here. It's all my fault for bursting in on you like this, and I plead for your forgiveness."

"There's nothing to forgive, Elizabeth," Jessie assured her guest. "I'm delighted that you've come early. This way the three of us will have some time to chat before everyone else arrives."

"You are always so gracious, my dear," Elizabeth gushed, patting Jessie's hand. "You turn a social blunder into a blessed event, if you'll forgive that last rather inappropriate phrase."

Taking both of her guests by the hands, Jessie led them over to where a bar had been set up and was being tended by Carlos.

"What will you have, Elizabeth, Stan?"

A few minutes later, when both Birkenhalls had drinks in their hands, the trio stood near the bar listening to the music the orchestra had begun to play—a Viennese waltz, followed by something Germanic with much bluster to it.

"How have you been, Jessie?" a solicitous Birkenhall inquired as he twirled his glass of whiskey in both of his large hands.

"Fine, Stan, just fine. Did your herds winter well this year?"

"We lost nearly a score of steers to that blizzard that hit us during the last week in January, but other than that we came through the winter in pretty good shape."

"I'm glad to hear it," Jessie said as Elizabeth gripped her arm. Elizabeth whispered, "Did you know that Mary Lee Salton has run off with a *tinker*, of all possible persons?"

"No, I didn't," a surprised Jessie responded. "Her husband must be devastated."

"Jim Salton'll survive," Birkenhall declared. "He's been known to have something of a wandering eye himself."

"But a tinker!" his wife exclaimed, feigning shock, which could not hide the gossipy delight dancing in her wide eyes. "Can you *imagine*?"

Jessie was convinced that Elizabeth could very well imagine Mary Lee Salton locked in the hot embrace of a rough and rapacious traveling tinker, but she was saved from having to comment any further on the matter by Elizabeth's husband's sudden exclamation.

"Here he comes now—the guest of honor himself. Hello there, Ki. Happy birthday to you!"

Jessie turned to find Ki entering the great room, attired in a dark blue dress coat, over a white waistcoat, and gray trousers with a band of black braid running down the outer sides of both legs. His white evening shirt had a high closed collar and a stiff front adorned with a blue cambric bow tie.

Ki joined them, and Birkenhall, as they all exchanged pleasantries, vigorously pumped his hand. Elizabeth, with a simper, accepted Ki's kiss upon the back of her eagerly outstretched hand.

From the corner of her eyes, Jessie saw Esmeralda opening the front door to admit a flurry of men and women who were talking and laughing as they entered the room.

"If you'll excuse us . . . " Jessie, followed by Ki, left the Birkenhalls and went to greet the arriving guests.

It was some time before Jessie could manage to get Ki alone but, when she finally did, she lowered her voice and said, "I thought you were going to miss your very own birthday party."

"I almost did," Ki confessed and proceeded to tell her about his meeting with Carl Landsman and then with the two thieves who had stolen the remuda that had been in Landsman's charge.

"Will Carl be all right, do you think?" a concerned Jessie asked when he had completed his account of the encounter. "It sounds to me as if he was badly hurt."

"It was no love tap he got from one of those thieves, but as he said to me at one point, 'I've got a thick hide but a far thicker skull so I reckon I'll live.' "

"And you? Were you hurt?"

"I sustained a bruise or two but none bad enough to keep me away from this birthday party you were kind enough to give for me. Who's that lovely little thing over there by the windows? The one with the big brown eyes and bustle?"

"Never you mind who she is. That 'lovely little thing,' as you call her, happens to be engaged to be married to the gentleman on her right."

Ki sighed and pressed the back of his right hand to his forehead in a melodramatic gesture of despair. "Curses!" he moaned in the very best tradition of stage villains. "Foiled again!"

A woman swathed in silk and satin came cruising up to them. "Jessie, darling, how are you? Don't tell me, I know. You're wonderful. It shows in your ever-lovely face."

"How are you, Sarah?"

"I'd be fine if Ki would finally give in to my pleading and consent to marry me. I don't know how many times

26

I've asked him to do so, but he's a slippery little devil. He won't give me an answer, though I've promised him a bountiful dowry as part of the marriage contract. Oh, before I forget. Felicitations, birthday boy."

Ki grinned and winked at Jessie.

Sarah brought to her eyes the lorgnette she was carrying in her right hand and bent forward to peer at the brooch Jessie was wearing. "I do declare! What a perfectly splendid piece."

"Thank you," Jessie said as Sarah straightened and lowered her lorgnette.

"A gift from an admirer, I expect?"

"No, I'm afraid not."

Up again went Sarah's lorgnette, through which she peered quizzically at Jessie.

"It's been in the family for generations," Jessie explained to satisfy Sarah's curiosity. "My great-great-grandfather gave it as a gift to his bride-to-be. It has long been a treasured possession of the women in the Starbuck family."

"How very romantic."

Jessie realized that Sarah's response had been automatic and that the woman, though still peering through her lorgnette, was no longer peering at her. She turned her head and saw the young man who was standing just inside the door as he surveyed the guests gathered in the great room.

"You must tell me who that handsome devil is," Sarah said and sighed. "Or is he your little secret, Jessie?"

"I'm afraid I can't tell you who he is, Sarah."

"Aha! Then I was quite right, wasn't I? He *is* your little secret!"

"I can't tell you who he is," Jessie said, "for the simple reason that I don't know who he is."

Sarah spun around, her lorgnette forgotten, to stare at Jessie. "You don't know who he is? Then what in the world is he doing here at Ki's birthday party?" Before Jessie could answer, Sarah turned to Ki. "A friend of yours then?"

27

Ki shook his head. "Never saw him before in my life."

Sarah turned her attention back to the latest arrival. "A veritable Greek god, isn't he? Look at those shoulders. Look at those blue eyes and that lovely blond hair and mustache. Ki, I think I shall forsake you for him. He is really quite too good to be true. I haven't seen such a handsome man since my second husband died."

"Excuse me, Sarah," Jessie said. "I must mingle."

But Jessie didn't mingle. She went directly to where the newcomer was standing and said, "Good evening. I'm Jessica Starbuck. And you are . . . "

He stared at her without speaking. His blue eyes didn't blink and to Jessie they seemed like two lovely lagoons. He was, she told herself, even more handsome up close than he was when seen from a distance through clouds of cigar smoke that were beginning to fill the room.

He was taller than she was—six feet three, she estimated. Broad shoulders above a narrow waist and equally narrow hips. An aquiline nose as befitted a Greek god. Hair the color of honey and lips as sensuous as any she had ever before seen. She resisted the urge to touch them with her own. She *would* not make a fool of herself.

"I take it you won't tell me your name."

He seemed to snap out of a trance. "I beg your pardon? Oh. My name. Forgive me, Miss Starbuck, but you have only yourself to blame."

"I beg your pardon?"

He smiled then, and Jessie felt her knees grow weak and her heart begin to flutter.

"I mean, dear lady, that you have only yourself to blame for my being a ninny and not promptly answering your question. Your beauty quite overwhelmed me there for a moment. Although I had been told you were a beautiful woman, I was quite unprepared for just *how* beautiful you are. My name is James Barton." He bowed, took her hand and kissed it.

28

James Barton. The name echoed in Jessie's mind. She had never, to the best of her knowledge, heard it before. A friend of her father's perhaps? Not likely. She knew all her father's friends. Then who was James Barton?

"I'm a man of business, Miss Starbuck. I've been traveling through the West in search of investment opportunities."

Now that she knew who he was, what was he doing *here*?

"I happened to notice the article in the newspaper about this party and I recognized your well-known name immediately." His face fell.

"What is it, Mr. Barton? Is something wrong?"

"I have a terrible confession to make."

"You do?" Jessie asked, her curiosity piqued.

"I am a gate crasher."

He had told Jessie nothing she didn't already know. His confession and his boyish head hanging—she expected him to shuffle his feet at any moment—amused her. "I should have the servants show you the door," she said with mock sternness.

"I know I had absolutely no right to intrude—"

"That's correct; you did not have the right. But I am glad you were brash enough to do so." Jessie hooked her arm in his. "Come with me and I'll introduce you to my other guests."

Barton, breaking into a smile at the sight of Jessie's arm on his own, willingly accompanied her as she made her way to a group of guests who were engaged in an animated conversation not far away. She introduced Barton to each of them and was not unaware of the longing looks several of the ladies gave him.

"Mr. Barton is traveling in the area looking for suitable investment opportunities," she told Stanley and Elizabeth Birkenhall moments later when she introduced them to Barton.

"Oil," Birkenhall muttered through a mouthful of Esmeralda's *puchero*, which he had just forked into his mouth from his plate. "That's where the money's to be made. Oil. You mark my words."

"Will you be with us long, Mr. Barton?" asked an obviously entranced Elizabeth, the food on her plate forgotten as she stared at the young man standing next to Jessie.

"Not long, I'm afraid," he answered with a polite smile. "I have obligations back east and must return quite soon to see to them."

"What a shame," Elizabeth said, pursing her lips, and Jessie, glancing covertly at Barton's handsome profile, could only agree with her.

"Jessica, Jessica!"

She turned to find Sarah signaling to her with her lorgnette. Then Sarah was bearing down on her and Barton like a mare gone mad.

"Who—"

"A friend of mine," Jessie whispered to Barton. "Her name is—"

"Sarah Cummings," Sarah interrupted breathlessly as she joined Jessie and Barton and held out her hand to Barton. "I mean Wetherby. Cummings was my *first* husband's name. I'm in a bit of a dither, it would seem."

"I can't imagine why, dear," Jessie said sweetly as Barton bent and kissed Sarah's hand.

"How very European you are, sir. Jessie?"

Remembering her manners, Jessie introduced Barton to Sarah.

"Are you married, Mr. Barton?" Sarah bluntly asked him.

"No, I'm not."

"Engaged?"

Barton shook his head.

"How very *interesting*!" Sarah exulted with a mischievous glance at Jessie. "I, too, am unencumbered—I mean unmarried—since the sad passing of my second husband, Mr. Wetherby. Jessie, you must have so many things to do. Don't let James and I keep you from them, darling."

Jessie managed a smile and excused herself. She looked back over her shoulder on her way to the buffet table and barely succeeded in suppressing the laughter that bubbled up in her throat as she watched Sarah drag Barton into a corner. He tried but failed to maneuver his way out of her matronly clutches.

She spent the next ten minutes talking to her guests and keeping a secretive eye on Mr. James Barton, who was still hopelessly cornered by Sarah Wetherby.

"Ladies and gentlemen," called out the leader of the orchestra, and all heads turned toward him. Raising his baton, he said, "At this point in the festivities, it is time for a little divertissement."

His audience waited expectantly.

"Shall we play drop-the-handkerchief?" he asked.

"What in the world's that?" cried a perplexed man at the rear of the crowd.

"Oh, yes, let's!" a woman not far from him simultaneously cried. "It's ever so much fun!"

"I'll explain the game, if I may, to those of you who are not familiar with it," said the orchestra leader. "Everyone forms a circle, facing inward. The person who is 'it' carries a handkerchief—I'm sure one of the gentlemen will lend us his handkerchief for the event—and makes his way around the outside perimeter of the circle. When he drops the handkerchief behind the lady of his choice, she must seize it, chase him around the outside of the circle and catch him before he can reach the spot she vacated and occupy it. If she fails to do so, she becomes 'it' and must choose a gentleman to drop the handkerchief behind, and the process then repeats itself."

"Hold on a minute," Birkenhall grumbled. "That's not the way we played it in the part of Texas where I was born and raised with the yearlings."

"Sir?" said the orchestra leader somewhat testily.

"Where I come from, if the person behind whom the

31

handkerchief was dropped catches up to the person who dropped it before that person can get halfway around the circle to the empty spot left in it, he or she gets to collect either a kiss or a piece of candy. We always called that 'catch-a-kiss-or-candy.' "

"Candy," repeated the somewhat nonplussed orchestra leader, glancing at the buffet table.

"There's no candy to be found in this room," Birkenhall bellowed. He began to laugh. "That's the point of catch-a-kiss-or-candy. It's a way of getting halfway along to courting for those folks lucky enough to still be single."

He laughed even louder as his wife gave him an indignant poke in the ribs.

The orchestra leader, looking relieved about the matter of the missing candy, nodded and exclaimed, "A circle, ladies and gentlemen. Form a circle, if you please."

The guests eagerly complied with the request, and soon a huge circle had been formed in the great room.

"Who will volunteer to be 'it' this first time out?" inquired the orchestra leader.

"I will," James Barton volunteered, holding up his hand where he stood on the far side of the circle from Jessie. From his pocket he withdrew a white handkerchief neatly folded into a square, and then he stepped out of the circle, which closed behind him. As the band struck up a marching tune, Barton began to walk around the outside of the circle in measured strides.

Jessie told herself it didn't matter. It didn't matter one bit if he didn't drop the handkerchief behind her. It was, after all, only a game and a bit of a silly one at that, come to think of it. But, she ruefully admitted to herself, if James Barton didn't drop his handkerchief behind her—if he *dared* drop it behind Letitia Parker or perhaps Lottie Sloan, both of whom were as pretty as painted pictures—she would, she knew for a fact, simply *die*.

He was coming closer. She closed her eyes, hoping . . .

She didn't hear the sound of the soft cloth falling to the floor directly behind her, but she did hear two other things.

She heard the sound of running feet behind her and Ki's voice calling out, "Run, Jessie!"

She turned and ran after Barton, who was loping around the circle some distance ahead of her. Holding her skirts ankle-high with one hand, she chased him. She wasn't intent on catching him before he reached the spot in the circle she had just vacated. She had another, and to her more important, goal in mind. She intended to catch Barton before he could make his way halfway around the circle which would mean—

Catch-a-kiss-or-candy.

She became aware of people cheering her as she ran on. She caught a fleeting glimpse of Ki's face as she passed him. But her eyes were focused on Barton just ahead of her now.

Then her hand was upon his shoulder. He halted and, smiling like the cat who has just swallowed the canary, turned to face Jessie, who was out of breath but, like him, smiling.

As the party guests applauded Jessie's capture, she whispered to Barton, "You didn't run very fast at all."

"I didn't, did I?" He took her in his arms and kissed her.

The applause of the onlookers grew louder, but Jessie didn't hear it, lost as she was in Barton's embrace and drowning in the sensations his lips were awakening by pressing on hers. For a long moment, the world went away from her and there was only James Barton—his lips, his hard body pressing against her own, crushing her breasts . . .

Then, too soon, it ended. She withdrew from Barton's embrace, someone called out, "You're still 'it,' mister," and she returned to her place in the circle as Barton again began to stalk around the outside of the circle. This time he dropped the handkerchief behind Sarah Wetherby, who let out a little cry of unadulterated delight and went racing after the young man with the speed of a gazelle despite her body's bulk.

Jessie, along with many others, clapped when Barton, even fleeter of foot than was Sarah, managed to reach and occupy the space in the circle Sarah had held.

She, her bosom heaving, pursed her lips in a frustrated pout. When Barton saw her expression, he took her in his arms, bent her over backward, and planted a passionate kiss on her lips.

When he raised her up and let her go, she whooped wordlessly and then cried, "This is the best game I've played since my last hand of strip poker!"

Hours after the game had ended, the first of the guests left the party. Jessie and Ki, flanking the front door, bade them good-bye after thanking them for coming. Then there were songs, which everyone joined in singing, and finally, a rowdy rendering of "Happy Birthday" and a toast to Ki.

The guests began then to leave in twos and threes, and soon there was left only Sarah Wetherby, who had become, Jessie noticed, a bit tipsy.

"Lovely party," she enthused and downed the brandy in her snifter. "Enough of that poison," she declared, putting down her glass. "Puts on the pounds faster than a twister hits town."

Jessie whispered to Ki, who went outside to tell Carlos's son, Carlito, to bring Sarah's carriage around to the front of the house.

"Where did everybody go?" Sarah inquired to Jessie as she looked around the empty room. "Where did *he* go?"

"Where did who go?" Jessie asked, although she was quite sure she knew who Sarah had in mind.

"James Barton, that's who. Don't tell me you let him escape, Jessie?"

"I never saw him leave, to tell you the truth. He must have left when I wasn't looking."

"He's a slick so-and-so, that one. He certainly must be,

34

because *I* was looking all the time!"

Sarah and Jessie both burst into delighted laughter.

They were still laughing when Ki returned to tell them that Sarah's carriage was out front and ready for her.

"You'll be able to drive, won't you?" Jessie asked as Sarah took several unsteady steps toward the door.

"Of course I will," was Sarah's confident answer. "And if it turns out I can't drive, there's still nothing to worry about. My horse would know the way home blindfolded. Good night, all."

Ki took Sarah's arm and escorted her to her carriage. He watched her drive off, her hands surprisingly steady on the reins, and then he reentered the house to find Jessie yawning and stretching.

"It was a fine party," he told her. "But it seems to have tired you out."

"It wasn't the party that tired me out. It was burning the midnight oil last night over my account books that did that. I should have known better than to stay up so late the night before a party."

"Thanks, Jessie."

She looked at him. "Thanks for what? The party?" When he nodded, she said, "Don't thank me for doing something you deserved and I enjoyed doing."

Ki became aware that something was bothering him. As Carlos cleared the bar and Esmeralda began to remove the leftover food from the buffet table and carry it back to the kitchen, he stood there trying to pinpoint exactly what it was. He looked around the room. It wasn't the misplaced furniture the guests had rearranged to suit themselves or the guttering candles about to go out that disturbed him. Nor was it the movements of the two servants as they worked to clear the room of the remains of the party's food and drink.

Then . . . what?

"Ki, if you'll excuse me, I think I'll go straight to bed."

35

"Go ahead, Jessie." Ki's eyes roved to the windows, to the front door . . .

Jessie came up to him and placed her hands on his shoulders.

He looked at her and smiled as she kissed him chastely on the forehead.

"Sweet dreams," she murmured and started to turn.

He gripped her arm, preventing her from leaving. "Jessie—"

"Yes?"

"What did you do with the Firebird?"

"What did I do with it?" Her right hand rose to her decolletage. She looked down. Her mouth opened, but she didn't—couldn't—speak for a moment. Then, staring at Ki, she said, "It's gone."

"You didn't put it back in your jewel box at some point during the party?"

"No, I didn't. It must have come unclasped and fallen to the floor." Jessie made a swift circuit of the room as she searched for her lost brooch. "I don't see it. Ki, help me look for it, will you?"

Ki had needed no invitation to join the search; he was already moving pillows on sofas and pushing chairs aside to look beneath them.

"Esmeralda!" Jessie called, and when the woman had come in from the kitchen, she asked her to help search for the Firebird.

"Do not worry," Esmeralda assured her as she moved the floor-length draperies on the windows to look beneath them. "We will find it."

But a thorough search by all of them, including Carlos, who joined the hunt late after returning from the wine cellar, was unsuccessful. The brooch remained among the missing.

"Look in the *puchero*, Esmeralda," Jessie ordered.

"But it could not be in—"

36

"Do as I say!" Jessie demanded angrily and then quickly apologized for her outburst and explained, "I ate some of the stew during the evening. When I was bending over to spoon it from the dish my brooch might have fallen unnoticed into it."

Esmeralda left the room. When she returned, she stood stiffly in the doorway and shook her head. "I looked in the *puchero*, in the salad bowl, in every dish. It is not in any of them."

The search continued. Old ground was gone over again. And again. Without success.

Jessie, close to tears, threw herself into an overstuffed chair and stared up at Ki. "I feel as if I've lost part of myself. That brooch—it is not its monetary value that matters to me, although it is worth thousands. It has a far greater sentimental value. Oh, Ki, what do you suppose has happened to it? Where do you suppose I lost it?"

Ki hesitated a moment, not wanting to add to Jessie's distress, but then said, "Maybe you didn't lose it. Maybe it was stolen."

"But how . . . who . . . "

Before Jessie could complete her question a memory flared in her mind. A memory of James Barton pressing her to him, his hard body crushing her breasts . . .

"It could only have been stolen by someone who was very close to me tonight—*if* it has been stolen," she said softly. "The only person who was close enough to me tonight to unclasp and steal the brooch was—"

"James Barton, gate crasher," Ki said.

Jessie, fighting back tears, could only nod.

Chapter 3

Jessie lay awake in her bed as the minutes and then the hours of the night passed. She twisted and turned, tried this position, then that position. But nothing she did would encourage sleep to come to her.

Finally she gave up trying and lay there, staring at the ceiling she could not see in the dark, and thought about the Firebird.

She, Ki, Carlos, Esmeralda and even Carlito had searched again for it throughout the entire house before finally giving up and going to bed. They had turned the house upside down and still none of them had found it. Even as they searched, Jessie knew that their efforts would prove to be fruitless, and they were. The memory of James Barton's kiss, the memory of his body pressing against her own, was all she could think about. But now the thought brought her no pleasure, only pain. Because even before the final search for the Firebird had ended, she was convinced in both her heart and mind that the brooch would not be found. She was certain that Barton had somehow managed to steal it from her during their embrace.

She felt violated. She felt almost as if she had been raped. She also felt guilty, as if it had been her fault that the jewel had vanished. As she lay there in the hot dark, she went over again the events of the night, trying to discover whether she had done anything that might have contributed to the loss of the brooch that she considered priceless in terms of its sentimental value. But she could come to no clear conclusion. Even so, she silently chastised herself for not having been more careful.

And yet how could she have known that Barton—that anyone—would attempt to steal the treasure from her? The answer was that she could not have known. There was no way for her to have known. The people at the party, after all, had been her close friends and, in some cases, business associates.

Except for James Barton, about whom she knew next to nothing. What was it he had told her? That he had been traveling in the West in search of investment opportunities. Those had been his exact words, as she recalled. She frowned in the darkness. But there was something else he had said. Something about having read about the party in the local newspaper, the *Clarion Call*. He had said that he had noticed and recognized her name in the article.

Jessie suddenly sat bolt upright in bed. She remembered reading the article herself. It had mentioned the fact that she would be wearing the Firebird. She had told the reporter who had visited her so. She had explained to the woman, as she recalled, that the jewel had been passed down to successive generations of Starbuck women. The reporter had noted that fact in the article, Jessie recalled. Anyone reading the piece would have known that the Firebird was worth a great deal of money.

Had James Barton come to the party with the specific purpose of attempting to steal the Firebird? There was no way to know, not for sure there wasn't. But Jessie's suspicions concerning him had grown steadily stronger ever since Ki had first mentioned the possibility that the brooch might have been stolen.

She got out of bed and went to the open window, through which a cool breeze was blowing. But the breeze could not cool her flushed face or body as she stood there while anger surged within her—an anger directed at the thief, whoever it was, who had robbed her of her highly prized possession.

Take care, she warned herself. You don't know for a fact that the brooch was stolen. No, I don't, she thought. But what I do know is that I am going to town first thing in the morning. I am going to find James Barton, and somehow or other, I am going to find out whether or not he stole the Firebird from me.

Jessie was seated at the kitchen table, a cup of coffee cradled in her hands, when Ki came into the room, which was filled with the light of the rising sun.

They exchanged greetings, and then Jessie told him that she was convinced that James Barton had stolen the ruby brooch from her.

"He told me he had read about your birthday party in the newspaper," she continued. "The Firebird was prominently mentioned in that article."

"I know. I read the piece. But that's a pretty flimsy basis on which to accuse Barton of the theft, if you don't mind my saying so." Ki made himself a cup of tea and joined Jessie at the table. "I had a thought during the night that might explain the Firebird's mysterious disappearance."

Jessie gazed expectantly at him over her coffee cup.

"It may very well have come unclasped and fallen from your gown without your having noticed it doing so."

"But we searched everywhere and it simply isn't here. It couldn't have simply vanished into thin air!"

Ki held up a hand. "Hear me out. What I was going to suggest is this. Suppose you did lose it. Then suppose further that someone at the party found it and kept it."

"I've known the people who were at the party for years in all cases but one. That one case is James Barton. No, Ki,

40

I'm sure none of my friends or business associates would have done what you're suggesting."

"It is, however, a possibility, you'll have to admit."

"I agree that it's a possibility, but it is hardly what I would call a probability."

Ki drank some of his steaming tea. "There is a second possibility not dissimilar to the one I just proposed. Suppose it was one of the servants who found the brooch during our searches last night. Suppose that person kept it and pretended not to have found it."

Jessie shook her head as she refilled her cup with coffee. "I don't believe for one minute that Esmeralda or Carlos would do such a thing. Both of them are as honest as the day is long."

"What about Carlos's son? He participated in the last search we made."

"Carlito? I don't think he would do such a thing either. No, Ki, I'm convinced that it was James Barton who stole the brooch. Probably at the time we embraced during the drop-the-handkerchief game. He admitted to me that he had read about the party in the newspaper, so he had to have known that I would be wearing the Firebird. I think that's the one and only reason he came to the affair—to steal my brooch. That would explain why he made himself scarce later. I don't recall having seen him after the game ended, do you?"

"No, now that I think about it, I didn't."

"He didn't even bother to say good night."

"What do you plan to do?"

"Talk to Barton."

"How do you know you can find him?"

"I don't know if I can, but I certainly intend to try."

"He may already be far away from here," Ki pointed out. "Especially if your suspicions are correct."

"Are you suggesting I not try to locate and question him?"

"No, I'm not. As a matter of fact, I plan to go with

41

you in case there's trouble. If Barton did indeed steal the brooch, he might very well take rash action against you if you confront him as you're planning to do."

"I'm not going to town unarmed," Jessie said pointedly. "I intend to take my derringer."

After a breakfast of flapjacks and sausages, she and Ki drove into town.

"How do you want to go about this?" he asked her as they turned a corner onto the town's main street, which was clogged with traffic, most of it commercial.

"I thought we'd begin by checking the boarding houses and hotels in town to see if Barton is staying at one of them."

"Good idea. But I'd try the hotels first if I were you. That might save us some time. Barton, judging by his fashionable clothes and good grooming, didn't strike me as a man who would buy for himself anything but the best. I think he would have stayed at the finest hotel in town and not at a lesser one. Certainly not at a boarding house."

"Then we'll go to the Empire first." Jessie drove on, made a left turn onto Prince Street and parked the carriage in front of the Empire Hotel.

Ki followed her into the hotel's lobby and stood beside her as she spoke to the desk clerk.

"I'm looking for a gentleman whose name is James Barton," Jessie told the clerk. "I thought he might have registered at your hotel."

"Barton? James Barton?" The elderly clerk cocked his head to one side, stroked his whiskered chin and then shook his head. "I'm sorry, but we have no one registered under that name."

"You're sure?" Ki prompted.

The clerk gave him a disdainful look. "Have a look at our ledger, if you doubt my word."

Ki and Jessie both examined the open ledger the clerk turned around and shoved toward them. They leafed through

42

its pages, checking all the names and the dates written next to them.

"No James Barton," Jessie remarked when they had finished.

"Just so," said the desk clerk somewhat snidely and reached for the ledger.

"Just a minute, if you please," Ki said, holding onto the ledger. "Look, Jessie. There are two men registered on their own. One on the eighteenth of this month and the other on the twentieth."

"Are you thinking that 'James Barton' may be an alias?"

Instead of answering Jessie's question, Ki spoke to the clerk. "The man we're looking for is tall, well built and in his late twenties or early thirties. He has broad shoulders, blue eyes, blond hair and a blond mustache. Do you have a guest who fits that description?"

"We do."

"His name?" Jessie asked.

"Simon Pettigrew."

Ki glanced at Jessie as his finger pointed to the name, which was one of the two he had noticed during his earlier examination of the ledger. Simon Pettigrew had registered at the hotel on the twentieth of the month.

"Is Mr. Pettigrew still registered at the hotel?" Jessie inquired.

"He is, yes."

"Thank you very much," Ki said, noting the room number listed next to Simon Pettigrew's name. "We're much obliged to you." As they left the desk, he said to Jessie, "He's in room number five. You want to pay him a visit—if he's there?"

"You bet your boots, I do!"

They climbed the staircase that led to the second floor and found room number five at the end of a long corridor. Jessie rapped smartly on the door.

43

They waited. No answer. She knocked again, louder this time. Still no answer.

Ki tried the door. Locked. "Pettigrew!" he called out. No reply. "We could camp in the lobby and wait for him to show up," he suggested.

They made their way back downstairs, where Ki said, "Wait here. I'll be right back." He crossed the lobby and went to the desk. When he returned moments later, he told Jessie, "I asked the clerk if he knew of Mr. Barton's—pardon me—Mr. Pettigrew's whereabouts, and he told me that the man might be found in the Palace Saloon. He claims our man, whatever his real name is, spends a great deal of time in such establishments. Shall we go?"

They drove to the Palace and once inside spotted Barton holding forth in a corner of the room where a crowd had gathered around him. They joined the crowd and saw that their quarry was busily engaged in conducting some sort of gambling game that involved three small boxes.

"Step up close, gentlemen," he intoned, beckoning to the men watching, whose eyes were all on the three boxes that rested on the bare top of a small table. "Try your luck again, but I must be fair and warn you that the hand is quicker than the eye. By that I mean—I am an eminently fair man, gentlemen—that *my* hand is quicker than *your* eyes."

Jessie and Ki moved closer to the table along with the men surrounding them.

Barton held up a penny, a newly minted one, that caught the light and glittered. "I shall place this penny—" His eyes fell on Jessie. He stopped speaking and stared at her, his mouth open, his eyes wide. Then, swallowing hard, he laughed nervously and said, "Gentlemen, you will have to excuse me for a moment. I have some urgent business to attend to. But I assure you that, the moment it is finished, I shall return and the game will begin again and you will all, each and every one of you, have the chance to win and win big. That is a promise."

Barton pocketed his penny and shouldered his way through the crowd that was grumbling about the delay in the gaming.

"My dear Miss Starbuck," he exclaimed, "what a pleasant surprise to see you again. I hardly expected to and certainly not in this notorious den of iniquity."

"Mr. Barton—or Pettigrew or whatever your real name is," Jessie said sharply, "do you recall the ruby brooch I was wearing at last night's party?"

Barton's face paled. "I do. But what—"

"I might as well come directly to the point," Jessie stated. "In addition, I might as well be quite frank in what I have to say to you. My brooch disappeared last night and I suspect that you stole it from me."

"How did you know about the name Pettigrew?"

Ki answered Barton's question. "A simple matter of checking with the desk clerk at the Empire Hotel, who recognized your description when I gave it to him, sir. He identified you for us as the man who had registered at the hotel under the name Simon Pettigrew."

"You remember my friend Ki," Jessie said, "in whose honor the party was given last night."

"Miss Starbuck, I can explain. I did not attempt to deceive you last night. My name actually is James Barton. But I use the name Simon Pettigrew in most instances when I am traveling, in order to throw my competition off the track."

"Your competition?" Ki asked.

"Yes. You see, I am a businessman, as I believe I mentioned to Miss Starbuck last night. As such, I try to stay one step ahead of my competitors. But if they were to learn that James Barton is present in such-and-such a place and inquiring about—oh, let us say mineral rights—why, they would soon all be swarming onto the scene and my chances of arranging a profitable investment for the clients I represent would undoubtedly be spoiled. You do understand?"

Jessie, frowning, glanced at Ki. Then to Barton, she said, "About my ruby brooch."

"I am sorely disappointed to think, Miss Starbuck, that you would consider me a thief. I hasten to assure you that your suspicions are totally without foundation. Ordinarily I would take umbrage at such an accusation, but I cannot do so in this particular instance because I recall that the newspaper article I read about your party mentioned that the brooch you say has been stolen from you was a prized family heirloom, so I can understand that you are upset about its loss."

Jessie realized that she was not as sure now of her suspicions as she had been only moments earlier.

"I have not led an entirely exemplary life, Miss Starbuck," Barton continued, "but I am not a thief. It pains me to think that you suspect me of making off with your jewelry. I did no such thing. Why, when would I have had an opportunity to do so?"

"When we embraced during the drop-the-handkerchief game," Jessie answered.

Barton gave her a slow, sultry smile. The light flashed on his even white teeth as it had earlier on his bright new penny. "At the risk of offending you, I must say that it was not theft I had on my mind at that perfectly lovely moment."

Jessie blushed and found it hard to meet Barton's direct gaze.

"Perhaps we can go somewhere and talk," he suggested. "This is hardly the place—"

"You have business matters to attend to, I believe," Ki observed. "We wouldn't want to interfere with them."

It was Barton's turn to blush. "I'm afraid you've caught me out. I told you earlier that I have not led an exemplary life. Well, that is all too true, unfortunately. I number gambling among my vices."

"Let's go, Pettigrew!" a surly male voice bellowed from behind Barton. "Give us a chance to win back some of the

46

money we've lost to you so far."

Barton spread his hands, palms upward, in a gesture of helplessness. "I shall rejoin you in a moment, Miss Starbuck, if it should please you to wait upon me. Then we can discuss the matter that concerns you in more detail."

When Barton had returned to his table, Ki said, "I don't believe a word he says. He's got too many stories to tell with too many twists and turns to them."

"I'm not sure what to believe at this point."

"I think I'd like to take a look around that fellow's hotel room. Will you be all right if I leave you here alone with him?"

Jessie patted the pocket of the fringed buckskin jacket she was wearing. "I told you I was going to bring my derringer. You're going to look for the Firebird in Barton's room?"

"If he has it—that's one place it's liable to be. If it's not on him. Anyway, it's a place to start."

"I'll wait here for you. If I have to leave for any reason, I'll leave a message for you with the bar dog. Be careful."

When Ki had gone, Jessie moved closer to the table, where Barton was pointing to the three boxes on its surface and saying, "Now, then, gentlemen, I believe you all know how the game is played—"

"I don't," a burly black-eyed man said, pushing his hat back on his head. "Show me." He fingered a livid welt on his right cheek and licked his thick lips.

"It's simple, Lomax," said the thin man standing next to the one who had just interrupted Barton. "What you do is—"

"Your friend is quite correct, Mr. Lomax," Barton, interrupting, said smoothly. He reached into his pocket and came up with his penny. He held it up to glint in the light. "Now this penny—I take it and place it—are you watching closely, Mr. Lomax? I take it and place it inside this box."

Barton picked up one of the three boxes, opened it, closed and shook it so that it rattled. Then he put the box down

47

between the other two boxes. "Mr. Lomax?"

Lomax looked up from the boxes to stare at Barton, who said, "You know which box contains the penny, do you not?"

Of course he does, Jessie thought. A person would have to be blind not to know which box contains the penny.

"That one." Lomax put out a blunt finger and touched the box in the middle of the set of three. "The one that rattled."

"Right you are," Barton said. "Now, Mr. Lomax, I will rearrange the boxes, and when I have finished doing so you will be at liberty to tell me which box contains the penny. But before I do that, please place your bets."

Lomax bet five dollars after which Barton, with a wink at Jessie, bent over his boxes and, using both hands, rapidly shifted their positions on the table.

Jessie watched him closely, trying to keep track of the box she believed contained the penny. Barton's hands were a pale blur as they moved gracefully across the table top. Jessie, watching them, recalled their touch on her body, their warm and welcome touch . . .

Then, remembering why she was here, she blinked the memory away.

The three boxes now sat motionless on the table top.

Barton stood with his arms folded across his chest. "Well, Mr. Lomax? Which box contains the penny?"

"That one," Lomax said without hesitation, pointing to the box on the right.

Barton sighed. "Gentlemen, we have with us tonight a man with the keen eye of an eagle." He picked up the box Lomax had indicated and shook it. It rattled.

Lomax, grinning, accepted the congratulations of his bony companion and then the five dollars that Barton handed him. He added another five dollar bill to it and placed them both on the table.

"Mr. Lomax bets ten dollars, gentlemen," Barton said as he began to shuffle the boxes.

Jessie watched his movements carefully. When his hands were once again still, she chose the box in the middle.

Lomax chose the box on the left.

Again, Barton sighed and handed Lomax ten dollars.

Lomax placed the money with the ten already on the table, once again doubling his bet. He gave his companion a self-confident smile and then gestured impatiently at Barton to get on with the game.

"Watch closely, gentlemen. Will Mr. Lomax bankrupt me or will my hand finally deceive his eye this time around? Abracadabra, *zoom!*" Barton withdrew his hands from the boxes.

Lomax pointed to the middle box.

Jessie had chosen the same box.

Barton shook it. It made no sound. This time the gambler's sigh was one of relief. "Well, Mr. Lomax, a man can't expect to win every time."

Lomax watched Barton pick up the twenty dollars and pocket it. He muttered something to the man standing beside him and then said to Barton, "I'll bet another twenty I can beat you at your own game."

"You are a man of courage and perseverance, Mr. Lomax," Barton crooned as the money was placed on the table and he shifted the boxes in a small whirlwind of movement.

"That one!" Lomax barked, tension in his tone, and pointed to one of the boxes.

"That one, Mr. Lomax?" Barton raised an eyebrow. "Are you quite sure that is the one that contains the penny?"

Instead of answering the question, Lomax reached out and picked up the box he had indicated and shook it. It did not rattle. He slammed it down on the table, turned and stalked away, his companion hurrying along behind him.

When Ki arrived on foot at the Empire Hotel, he did not enter the building. If he went inside and upstairs to Barton's room, he reasoned, there was no way he could get inside, short of breaking down the door, which would not only attract unwanted attention but also might get him arrested for breaking and entering.

Not that he had any objections to breaking and entering. He did, however, have objections to being caught in the act. So he made his way through an alley that ran between the hotel and a dry goods store to the back of the building.

Once there, he carefully surveyed the area. There were two vertical tiers of windows, one on either side of the building. There was a back door. Above it was a tar-papered overhang. At one corner of the building sat a rain barrel.

Ki went to the barrel, carried it back to the overhang and turned it upside down. He climbed up on it and grasped the overhang with both hands to boost himself up. Then, standing on his toes, he reached upward and just barely managed to get a grip with the tips of his ten fingers on the sill of the first window in the vertical row on the right. He tried pulling himself up to it but failed to do so. Reconsidering the matter, he let go of the window sill, crouched in a bent-knee position on the overhang and sprang upward.

He caught the sill and his feet scraped the wall of the building. The momentum of his upward spring allowed him to climb up onto the sill and then through the open window into Barton's room. He dusted off his hands, hitched up his jeans, and began to make a systematic search of the man's room.

He opened bureau drawers and dumped their contents onto the floor. He moved the single picture on the wall, but there was nothing behind it. He stripped the bed and then carefully examined the mattress and pillow for any sign that Barton might have hidden Jessie's brooch in them. He found no such sign.

He went to the closet and opened the door. He quickly searched the pockets of every coat and pair of trousers he found there. He ran his fingers along the seams of every garment, searching for a hiding place where Barton might have stashed the jewel. He thrust a hand into each of Barton's shoes, which he found on the closet floor, and he checked the interior of a derby hat he found on a shelf.

He looked into the pitcher on the top of the bureau and found that it contained only water. He got down on his hands and knees and searched among the jumble of handkerchiefs, underwear, shirts and socks he had emptied out of the bureau drawers in case the brooch had been wrapped in one of them. He found nothing.

Rising and trying to suppress his sense of frustration, he looked around the room. There was nowhere the brooch could be that he hadn't searched. He stood there, hands on hips, as his eyes roamed about the room. Had he missed something? Was there a potential hiding place that he had overlooked?

He went to the bed and tried to unscrew the cast-iron cherubs perched on the bed's posts, but all four were rusted in place and thus offered no hiding place for a stolen jewel.

The word *failure* was an ugly bird that flew about the room and mocked him. Well, he had done his best. He went to the window. As he was climbing out of it, he thought that he and Jessie might have come too late. Perhaps Barton had already disposed of the Firebird. He could have sold it to someone—or it could be that he had never stolen it in the first place.

Which in turn meant—

Ki blocked the thoughts that rushed through his mind by concentrating instead on getting safely down, first to the overhang and then, with the help of the upended rain barrel, to the ground.

Having done so, he made his way through the alley and headed for the Palace Saloon.

When he arrived, he found Jessie waiting for him just inside the door.

"I was so worried about you," she said when she saw him. "I thought Barton might catch you in the act of ransacking his room."

"You mean he's not here?"

"No, he's not. He left some time ago."

"Where did he go, do you know?"

"No, I don't. But, as I said, I was afraid he would return to the hotel and find you in his room. Did you find my brooch? Was it in his room?"

"If it was, I couldn't find it."

Jessie's face darkened. "If it's not in his room—"

"I didn't say it wasn't in his room. I said I couldn't find it there."

"If it isn't there, then Barton must have it on him."

"Not necessarily. He could have disposed of it by now."

"Disposed of it?"

"Sold it to someone, for example."

"Oh, no!"

"It seems to me at this point that there's only one thing left for us to do and that is to find Mr. Barton and search *him*."

"We know at least one place to look for him."

They left the saloon together and made their way back to the hotel, where they climbed the stairs to Barton's room. Ki knocked on the door.

"Did you hear that?" Jessie asked.

"It sounded like someone groaning." Ki tried the door and found it unlocked this time. "Stand aside, Jessie." When she had moved to the left, he cautiously opened the door and stepped to the right.

The groaning was louder now.

Without stepping directly into the doorway, Ki peered into the room and saw Barton lying with his eyes closed on the floor. With Jessie right behind him he entered the room and went over to where Barton lay with one hand covering a bloody hole in his chest.

52

"Barton," Ki said and gently touched the man's shoulder.

Barton opened his eyes. "What happened?" Ki asked him. "Who did this to you?"

"Stabbed," Barton said through dry lips. "Thirsty."

Jessie quickly went to the bureau and filled a glass with water. She brought the glass to Barton, knelt beside him and gave the glass to Ki, who raised Barton's head and helped him drink.

Barton gagged, spilling some of the water.

"Miss Starbuck," he wheezed then, as he recognized Jessie. "I'm afraid I'm in no condition to receive guests."

"What happened?" she asked him, repeating Ki's question.

"Lomax followed me when I left the saloon. I didn't know he was after me. He wanted to get back the money I won from him. He got it."

"This man, Lomax," Ki said. "He was the one who stabbed you?"

"I'd already given him all the money I had on me. More— much more—than he lost to me. He said he meant to teach me a lesson—to teach me not to fleece other men like him. I'm afraid I learned the lesson he taught all too well, as you can plainly see. It is the last lesson I'll learn in what little is left of my life."

"You're dying, Barton," Ki said. "I take it you know that."

"I know that."

"Then it's time to wipe your slate clean. Did you steal Miss Starbuck's ruby brooch at the party last night?"

Barton's eyes closed. A soft sigh left his lips. "Yes," he said. "I did."

Jessie, a look of triumph on her face, glanced at Ki. "Where is it?" she asked.

"I read about your party in the newspaper," Barton said, his eyes still closed. "I think I told you that last night. When

I read about the brooch I decided to try to steal it. I would, I thought, be able to sell it for a pretty penny. But that was not to be."

A twisted smile played briefly across Barton's features. He focused his eyes on Jessie. "I am not what I said I was. I am not a businessman. I am not traveling through the West looking for investment opportunities for any clients. I am, simply put, a crooked gambler and a petty criminal, nothing more.

"When we played drop-the-handkerchief at the party— that's when I saw my chance. I stole not only a kiss but the Firebird as well while I held you in my arms, Miss Starbuck. Of the two, as I look back now, I do believe the kiss was more precious than the jewel."

"Where is it, Barton?" Ki demanded.

"Somebody was in my room—searched it," a distracted Barton murmured, opening his eyes and looking around him. "They were looking for something."

"I was looking for the brooch, Barton," Ki said and squeezed the man's shoulder to keep him from drifting off. "I didn't find it."

"You didn't find it," Barton said in a voice that was barely audible, "because it wasn't here. It was in my pocket."

Ki started to put a hand into one of Barton's trouser pockets.

"Too late," Barton whispered. As he did so, a thin trickle of blood emerged from between his lips and slid slowly down his chin. "It's gone."

"Gone where?" Ki asked, suppressing the urge to shake the whole story out of the dying Barton.

"Lomax found it on me. He took it. He called it a 'bonanza.' When he found it, he said this was his lucky day. The brooch—it didn't bring me any luck though. Maybe it will do better by him."

"Who is this Lomax?" Jessie asked anxiously.

"I never saw him before today when he gambled in the

saloon," Barton answered breathily.

"Barton—" Ki began but realized it was too late for any more questions.

Because Barton was dead.

Chapter 4

"Now what?" Ki asked, speaking more to himself than to Jessie as he stared down at the lifeless body of James Barton.

"Now," she solemnly said, "we have to find Lomax."

"Let's get out of here. There's nothing we can do for Barton. The only one who can do for him at this point is the coroner." Ki rose.

Jessie remained kneeling beside the corpse. She was surprised to find herself feeling only pity for Barton. True, the man had stolen her precious Firebird, but somehow she could no longer hate him for doing so as she had been doing up until the last few minutes of his life. There had then seemed to be something not only sorrowful about him but something altogether poignant. She recalled his remark about the kiss he had stolen from her being more precious than the ruby brooch he had also stolen.

"Jessie?"

"I wonder what he meant about having been a crooked gambler," she mused, not moving, her hands folded in her lap. "The game he was running in the saloon seemed honest enough to me."

"It was some sort of variation on the three shells and a pea game, am I right?"

"Yes. He put a penny in one of the three boxes, and the trick was to guess which box contained that penny after he had moved them about on the table. Lomax bet against him. He won too—at first. But then he began to lose. Each time Barton picked up the box Lomax had indicated and shook it and it didn't rattle, Lomax looked to be about ready to burst."

"I think I know now what Barton meant when he described himself as a crooked gambler." Ki searched through Barton's pockets until he found the three boxes the man had been using. He opened them all and showed Jessie that all three were empty.

"So?"

"Barton never did put the penny in any of these boxes."

"But I saw him put it in one of them!" Jessie protested.

"You *thought* you saw him do so." Ki checked the cuffs of Barton's frock coat. In the left one he found a bright, newly minted penny, which he held up for Jessie to see. "He palmed the penny instead of putting it in one of his boxes, and then he slipped it into his cuff."

"But if he did that— Ki, when Lomax first picked the box he thought the penny was in, Barton picked it up, shook it and the penny inside it rattled. I heard it. So what you say can't be true."

"Not necessarily. I saw this game run in Abilene one time. It was crooked as a dog's hind leg. I found out later, from the man who had run it, once he had gotten himself good and drunk and far too talkative. Do you happen to remember which hand Barton used to pick up the box that rattled?"

Jessie thought for a moment. "I believe it was—yes, it was his left hand. Every time Lomax won—that is to say every time the penny rattled inside the box Barton picked up after Lomax had selected it—he did so with his left hand."

"Which hand did he use to pick up and shake the boxes that didn't rattle?"

"His left—no, his right hand."

"There you have it."

"I don't understand. There I have what?"

Ki leaned over and pulled up the left sleeve of Barton's coat to reveal, strapped to the man's wrist, a small box like the three that had been in the dead gambler's pocket. He freed it, opened it and showed Jessie the ordinary dull penny it contained.

"Now I really am confused," she said, looking from the penny in the box to Barton to Ki.

"As I told you," he said, "Barton never put the new penny into any of the three boxes he was shuffling. Instead, he palmed it and dropped it into his coat cuff. When he wanted to let Lomax win in the beginning—that's how the game is played; it's how the gambler encourages a player to think he's on a lucky streak—he would pick up the empty box the bettor had chosen and shake it with his left hand. But it was the penny inside the hidden box strapped to his left wrist that rattled, not a penny in the box he had picked up. That box, like its two companions, was empty. When he wanted the bettor to lose, he simply switched hands. He'd pick up the box the bettor had selected—which was empty—with his right hand and shake it. Thus, no rattle."

"He really was a scoundrel, wasn't he?" Jessie said, a faint smile lifting the corners of her lips.

"By his own dying admission, yes, he was. Now, let's go see the marshal and tell him what happened here."

"There's been more killings in this town lately than a man can shake a stick at," the marshal, a keen-eyed man, complained. "Seems like folks do dote on doing each other in. It's the younger generation's doing most of it. They're not like we were at their age. They've got no respect for life or limb. You say the body of this Barton fella's over at the Empire?"

"Yes," Jessie answered.

"In room number five," Ki added.

"Well, we'll cart him over to the coroner's office, and if nobody lays claims to him, we'll bury him on Boot Hill at county expense." The marshal pulled a plug of tobacco from his pocket and bit into it. "You two didn't know the fella who killed the gambler, I take it?"

"We never saw him before today," Jessie explained. "But we heard him called Lomax."

The marshal almost choked on his chew. Coughing and sputtering, he leaned over and spit the tobacco into a brass spittoon that sat on the floor next to his desk. "Lomax, you say? You're telling me it was Bud Lomax did the dirty deed, are you?"

"The man who was with him just called him Lomax," Jessie declared.

"What'd this Lomax look like? A burly fella, was he?"

"Yes," Jessie said. "Over six feet tall and big in the chest and shoulders. He had black eyes and a scar on his cheek."

The marshal swore.

"What is it, Marshal?" Ki asked.

"That would be Bud Lomax, the fella you ran into. It's a dark day for this town when a man like that shows up on its doorstep."

"You know this Lomax?" Jessie prompted.

"Wish I didn't. He's more trouble than ten tomcats in heat, begging your pardon, Miss Starbuck. You name a crime, Bud Lomax has committed it. He's stolen cattle, had his way with unwilling women—he's a thoroughly bad apple, he is. Where'd you last see him?"

"Leaving the Palace Saloon," Jessie replied.

"Is he still in town?"

"I don't know. I haven't seen him since he was in the Palace."

The marshal thoughtfully stroked his stubbled chin. "Lomax is probably long gone from here by now. I hope and pray that's true. I don't fancy going up against a gunslick like him, I can tell you."

Jessie and Ki exchanged apprehensive glances.

"He generally stays pretty far to the south of us," the marshal continued. "Maybe he's gone back down there so that nobody will connect him with the killing. He probably left Barton for dead, not figuring he might live long enough to point the finger at him."

"You'll go after him, I suppose," Ki stated.

"Me?" The marshal looked annoyed. "No, sir, not me. If he's gone back down south to his regular stamping grounds, he's out of my jurisdiction. The law down there can look out for him. Of course, if I happen to run into him here in town, well, that's a horse of a different color."

"Where exactly can he be found when he's down south, do you happen to know, Marshal?" Ki inquired.

"Rumor has it that he goes to ground—when him and the men who ride with him aren't out raising hell and setting a chunk under it—somewheres down around Laredo. What's that to you? You aren't by any chance thinking of going after him to avenge the death of your friend Barton, are you?"

Jessie quickly shook her head in denial as Ki simultaneously said, "Not on your life, Marshal."

"Glad to hear it. You two don't look the least bit suicidal, so I figured you wouldn't want to tangle with that gun-hung hombre who'd just as soon shoot you as give you the time of day."

"How come you didn't tell the marshal about your stolen brooch?" Ki asked Jessie as they climbed into their carriage outside the man's office.

"I have the greatest respect for him," Jessie said, picking up the reins and moving her rig out, "but if word about my ruby brooch being stolen gets bandied about, there just might be more than the two of us trying get their hands on it."

"I see your point and it's a good one. An expensive item

like the Firebird would probably draw unsavory types to it the way honey draws flies."

He was silent for a time and then he asked, "Where are we going?"

"Back to the Palace. I want to make inquiries concerning Bud Lomax."

Once inside the saloon again, Jessie, followed by Ki, made her way to the bar and spoke to the man tending it.

"I'm looking for Bud Lomax," she told him. "He was in here earlier today. Would you by any chance know where he is now?"

"I don't know nobody named Lomax," the bar dog answered and then revealed his barefaced lie by asking, "Why would a respectable looking woman such as yourself be looking for an outlaw of that ilk?"

"So you do know Lomax," Ki commented.

The bar dog, apparently realizing the error he had made, shook his head vigorously. "I know the name, not *him*. I wouldn't know *him* if I fell over him."

Jessie put a hand into a pocket of her jeans. When it emerged, it held a gold eagle. She placed the coin on the bar. "That," she said, indicating the money with a nod, "will buy any information you have to sell about Bud Lomax."

"You won't tell anybody I talked to you about him?" the bar dog asked, leaning over the bar and glancing nervously up and down it.

Jessie shook her head and shoved the gold coin closer to the man.

"Fellow was in here a while ago. All excited, he was. Said he saw Bud Lomax and some skinny fellow riding out of town together. Said he saw blood on Lomax's clothes. Now, there was another fellow in here also not long ago. That fellow said the gambler who was running a game in here earlier wound up dead over in the Empire Hotel. Mind you, I'm not accusing anybody of anything. But it's been my experience in life that when you add up two and two

61

you wind up with four every single time."

"Which way did the first fellow you just mentioned say Lomax was heading when he left town with his sidekick?" Ki asked.

"South. But remember. I'm telling you what I heard. I ain't swearing to you it's true."

"Thank you," Jessie said as the bar dog picked up and pocketed the ten dollars she had placed on the bar in front of him.

Once outside and in their carriage, she drove away.

"We'll be heading south, I take it, after Lomax," Ki said nonchalantly as if he were commenting on the fine weather they were having.

"We are. Just as soon as we can change into trail clothes and put things in order at the ranch, we are."

Two days later, Jessie and Ki were scores of miles from the Starbuck ranch and heading southwest. Around her waist, Jessie now wore a cartridge belt. In its holster was her .38-caliber revolver, which was mounted on a sturdy .44 frame.

In Ki's saddle boot was a fully-loaded '73 Winchester, and in a pocket of his leather vest were six potentially deadly metal *shuriken*, or five-bladed throwing stars, any one of which could seriously wound or even kill a man.

The sun that blazed in the sky above them was wringing sweat from their bodies as well as from the bodies of the horses they rode.

Jessie's blood bay hung his head as he plodded on through the Concho-Colorado country, and Ki's black was slowing perceptibly.

Licking her dry lips to moisten them, Jessie said, "Let's head for those cedars over there to the right. We can dismount there and give the horses a rest."

"They need it. They need to get out of this sun, and so, by the way, do I." He untied the tan bandanna from around his neck and used it to wipe the sweat from his face.

Entering the shade of the cedars was a relief. The grove's relative coolness soothed both riders and their mounts.

Jessie slid out of the saddle and opened her canteen. She took off her Stetson, poured water into it and held the hat out for her horse to drink from. Ki followed her example and then sat down on the ground with his back braced against the stout trunk of a cedar, his knees up and his forearms resting on them.

Jessie took a drink of the warm water her canteen contained and then hunkered down next to Ki as the bay and black listlessly browsed the undergrowth nearby.

"We've lost the trail," a dispirited Jessie said, stating what had been unspoken between herself and Ki for the last few miles.

"We'll pick it up again."

Jessie wasn't so sure, but she didn't contradict her friend, whose optimistic statement was belied by the weary expression on his face.

"They veered west," Ki remarked, "so they could travel over that long stretch of rocky ground behind us. It's no wonder we lost track of them."

"Maybe we're being foolish to ride their backtrail—if we can find sign of them again."

"Foolish?"

"There are six of them now."

Ki and Jessie had seen the spot where the ground was torn up about fifteen miles to the north of their present location. The spot where a camp had been made and a fire built. The spot where horses had been grazed and which Lomax and the man riding with him had ridden into and then out of in the company of four men who had been in the camp. It had clearly been a rendezvous point.

"There are only two of us, Ki."

"That evens the odds. The two of us are an easy match for any number of desperadoes."

Jessie's smile, when it finally came, was wan.

63

"Seriously, though, do you have a plan in mind for when we catch up with Lomax and his riders?" Ki asked.

"I've been thinking about that. When we first started out, I suppose I had some vague notion of catching up with him and just accusing him of having killed Barton and stolen the brooch from him. But that was, I'm afraid, a foolish notion born of anger. We'll have to come up with something better than that if we don't want to find ourselves shot full of holes once we do catch up with Lomax and his men."

"We could always join his gang."

"Join his gang? You're not serious."

"Sure I'm serious. Like you said, we can't just say 'Hey there, Lomax, give us the brooch you took from Barton,' now can we?" Ki didn't wait for Jessie to answer him but plunged on, outlining the plan that he had been considering for some time as they rode southward. "If he'll let us ride with him—which means if we can convince him we're two hard cases just like him and his boys—then we've bought ourselves some time.

"Time to see how the land lies with the Lomax gang. We can keep an eye on Lomax and see if he's got the brooch. He's not likely to be closemouthed about it. Not when he's with his own men. He might have already told one or more of them about it. If that doesn't pan out, we can maybe get the man who was with him when he killed Barton to tell us what he knows about the brooch."

"It's something to consider," an obviously unconvinced Jessie mused. "I confess I've not been able to come up with anything better."

"You ready to move out?"

Jessie nodded and rose.

They looped the reins over their horses' heads, stepped into their saddles and continued their journey. Within minutes, they were out of the shelter of the cedars and once again exposed to the brutal sun that knew nothing of mercy. Soon the dark spots on the backs of their shirts began to spread. Sweat slid down their foreheads and into their eyes. The smooth cloth of their jeans clung to their damp legs. Their feet steamed in their boots.

The landscape began to change as they rode farther south and west. The hills flattened out and gave way to a seemingly endless plain that stretched before them as far as they could see.

As they rode on toward the ever-receding horizon, Ki drew rein and dismounted.

"What's wrong?" Jessie asked, slowing her horse.

"Nothing. Unless you consider hunger wrong." He bent down and pulled some spiral pods from a screw-bean mesquite plant. He gave a few to Jessie and then climbed back into the saddle. They ate the pods as they continued their journey.

"Smoke," Jessie observed some time later, pointing to the horizon.

"Could be a prairie fire."

They both kept their eyes on the thin mist of smoke rising in the distance, prepared to make a run for it if it turned out to be a prairie fire. But, as they drew closer to the smoke, they were able to see that it was rising from the ruins of a small house.

The building's stone chimney stood, a smoke-blackened monument to the fire that had destroyed all else. Chickens scratched in the dirt, and sitting on an overturned washtub was a woman whose back was bent and whose face was buried in her hands. Beside her stood a man, one of his hands resting on the woman's shoulder.

When he saw Ki and Jessie approaching, he pulled a knife out of the scabbard that hung from his leather belt.

"Hold on," Ki called out to him. "We mean you no harm."

The man assumed a fighting stance, the knife in his right hand raised defensively. "Don't you come any closer!" he shouted.

"Sir," Jessie said, "my friend told you the truth. We mean you no harm. We're just pssing through. If you attack us, we'll have to defend ourselves."

Ki surreptitiously fingered one of the deadly *shuriken* in his vest pocket.

The man slowly lowered his knife. He stood there, staring at Ki and Jessie, as tears formed in his eyes and rolled down his cheeks. The woman seated on the washtub rose and put her arms around him.

When Jessie and Ki had ridden up to the pair, she asked, "What happened to your house?"

"They burned it," the woman replied, stepping away from the man, her gaunt face filled with hatred.

"Who did?" Ki asked.

"Strangers," the man answered. "Six black-hearted drifters."

"There were six of them?" Ki gave Jessie a meaningful glance.

"They wanted food," the man said dully. "My wife, Clarissa, gave them some. They wanted to drink. We didn't have any. They said they'd settle . . . they laughed and said they'd settle for . . . "

Clarissa turned and put a silencing finger on her husband's lips. "It's over, John," she murmured. "We have to forget and go on."

"Can you forget what they did to you?"

"I will try to. I hope you will too."

Husband and wife embraced.

"Who were the men who . . . passed by here?" Ki asked.

"Never saw them before," John answered, his eyes ablaze. "If I ever see them again, I'll kill them!"

"Did one of them have a scar on his cheek?" Jessie asked. "Was he a big man?"

"You know him?" John asked, his eyes burning into Jessie's.

"The man did have a scar?" she persisted.

John nodded. "What are you two to him—to them?" His eyes shifted from Jessie to Ki.

"The man with the scar stole a valuable piece of jewelry from me," Jessie answered. "We've been trying to find him in order to get it back if we possibly can."

"You'll have to stand in line," John said.

"Beg pardon?" Ki said.

"Some Texas Rangers rode by here an hour or so after those beasts were here," Clarissa said. "We told them what had happened. They've gone after that bunch."

"We'll be on our way," Jessie said. "We're sorry for your trouble."

"You going to kill them if you catch them?" John asked.

"We'll do whatever we have to do to get back what belongs to the lady," Ki replied.

"I hope you kill them," John muttered. "I hope somebody does, you or the Rangers. I would have if they hadn't taken my rifle and run off my horse. I should have done it when they first rode up here, but I never thought . . ."

Clarissa tried with soothing words to comfort her husband, in whose eyes tears were once again welling.

Jessie and Ki wheeled their horses and began to follow the clear trail left by a group of riders, which led them in a southerly direction.

"Maybe they're heading for the border," Ki commented as they galloped along.

"They may very well be. The Rio Bravo's not all that many miles from here."

"If they do get across the border, that will leave the Rangers high and dry. They've got no legal right to cross over into Old Mexico after anybody, no matter what they might have done."

"The border won't stop us though," a grim-faced Jessie stated flatly.

The sound of shots being fired in the distance directly ahead of them spurred them on. Within minutes they spotted

Lomax and his men as they fled a pursuing group of three Rangers.

"Those lawmen are outnumbered," Ki commented.

"If they should happen to kill Lomax," Jessie said, "and that sure does look like what they're trying their best to do, we may never recover the Firebird."

"What do you mean?"

"I mean that Lomax might not have it on him. He might have given it to someone to keep for him. He might have hidden it somewhere for safekeeping. There's no telling what he might have done with it. I think we'd better keep those Rangers from killing him. We've got to do all we can—short of shooting a Ranger—to stop them from killing Lomax."

Ki gave Jessie a sidelong glance, but he said nothing.

"Can you think of a better way to make friends with Lomax," she asked him, "than to help him run off the law that's gunning for him? If we can help him do that, we have a good chance of becoming his friends for life. He'll be grateful to us for our help in getting the law off his trail. For maybe even saving his life if it comes down to that. He'll think—and we'll say—that we're on the wrong side of the law the same as he is. We'll tell him we want to throw in with him, and my guess is he'll welcome us with open arms. If he does, then we'll have ourselves a better than good chance in my estimation of finding the Firebird."

"Look," Ki said, pointing. "Lomax and his men are digging in. They evidently intend to stand and fight."

Jessie drew rein, signaling to Ki to do the same. Together they watched Lomax and his men, all of them out of their saddles now, take cover behind the trunks of some young mesquite trees and continue firing a steady volley of shots at the Rangers.

The Rangers turned their horses and retreated a short distance to avoid the punishing fire of the gang's desperate frontal attack. The lawmen drew rein and hit the ground running. Within seconds, they, too, had taken cover with one of their number gripping his horse's bridle and using the animal as a living breastwork.

"We could mount a flank attack against those Rangers," Ki suggested. "Maybe our efforts, combined with those of Lomax and his men, could drive them off."

"My thoughts exactly. You take the right flank; I'll take the left." Without another word, Jessie went galloping to the left, her side arm clearing leather as she did so.

She didn't stop until she had reached the left flank of the Rangers who were still battling the Lomax gang. She chose a spot where there was a shallow depression in the ground. She dismounted and assumed a prone position in the dip in the earth. Holding her .38 in both hands, she squeezed off a shot that went high—but still uncomfortably close—to the head of the lawman nearest her position. She was close enough to hear him swear and to see him shift position and take aim at the spot where she lay hidden from his sight.

"There's somebody on our left flank!" the startled man yelled.

Jessie heard the crack of a rifle and heard a Ranger beyond the one she had targeted yell, "Goddamn it, there's some son of a bitch on our right flank too!"

Jessie squeezed off a second round, which whined past the ear of the lawman she had targeted earlier. He swore and fired in her direction. His round went harmlessly over her lowered head.

The firing from Lomax and his men abruptly stopped as they evaluated their suddenly changed situation. But then one of the gang let out a yell and the firing resumed.

Jessie saw Lomax dart out from behind the tree where he had taken cover and move forward to another tree closer to the Rangers' position. She saw one of his men imitate his bold advance.

One of the lawmen let out a cry of rage followed by, "We got to get the hell out of here, or we're going to get ourselves blown to bits!"

Jessie, when she spotted one of Lomax's men about to fire at a Ranger who had unwittingly exposed his position, took aim at the gang member and fired. Her round caught him in the forearm, sending his arm jerking to the left and causing his gun to fall from his hand.

When she returned her attention to the Rangers, she saw that they were engaged in a frantic scramble for their horses.

She moved to her right so that she was facing Lomax's position at a sharp forty-five–degree angle. When he, seeing the Ranger's preparations for flight, moved out from behind the tree where he had taken cover and took aim at a lawman's back as the man tried to calm and mount his horse, she fired—at Lomax. He ducked back behind his tree. She hoped that he would think her shot, which had forced him back into a defensive position, had come from one of the Rangers' guns.

A volley of rifle shots sounded in the otherwise momentarily silent area. Ki's fusillade, though harmless, provided the final stimulus—if one was needed—that sent the Rangers galloping away from the spot, their spurs digging into the flanks of their mounts as they rode for their lives.

Laughter.

Jessie saw the laughing Lomax step out from behind the tree her round had forced him behind and stand there, his head thrown back, his gun still in his hand.

The men with him gradually emerged from the places where they had, like their leader, taken cover while they made their stand.

Jessie, her gun in her hand but aimed at the ground, stood up. As if her movement had been a signal, Ki moved into sight from behind the rotting stump of a dead mesquite tree.

Both of them, carrying their weapons, began to walk

70

toward the spot where Lomax stood, his gaze shifting back and forth between them.

"Who the hell are you two?" he barked as they halted a few feet from him.

"My name's Jessie."

"Ki."

"Jessie what?" Lomax asked. "Ki what?"

"Jessie and Ki—that's all you need to know," she said.

As Lomax's men gathered around him to study the new-comers, Lomax also squinted at them and said, "We could have run those lawdogs off without any help from you. But we're glad you took it upon yourselves to lend us a hand. It sure didn't hurt."

"Why?" asked a man standing beside Lomax.

"You want to know why we helped you out of a tough spot?" Jessie asked him.

"That's right," the man said in a decidedly suspicious tone of voice.

"That's easy enough to answer," Ki said. "Neither I nor Jessie have any love for lawmen. When we saw those three trying to put holes in your hides, we decided we just couldn't let that happen."

"Our only regret is that we didn't get to blow all three of them away," Jessie added.

Lomax laughed. "My, oh, my, but she's a mean woman, isn't she, Standish?" he said to the lean man at his side, who had been with him in the Palace Saloon.

"Not mean," Jessie corrected. "Just practical. In our business it's just a matter of good sense to put as many lawmen as possible out of commission."

"What *is* your business?" Standish asked.

"One that the law can't abide," Ki answered. "Which, without getting any more specific about it, is not unlike your business, I'd venture to say, judging by the fact that those Rangers seemed bound and determined to stop your clocks if they could."

71

"You know who we are?" Lomax asked, his eyes narrowing to thin slits.

"No more than you know who we are," Jessie answered smoothly.

"My name's Bud Lomax. Maybe you've heard of me?"

Jessie widened her eyes to simulate surprise. "You're the famous Bud Lomax?"

"None other."

Jessie whistled through her teeth. "I've heard of you. Who hasn't heard of the famous Bud Lomax? People talk about you and your exploits all over the Southwest. Let me shake your hand, Lomax. It's a real pleasure to meet you." As Jessie pumped a smiling Lomax's hand, she continued, "Ki, did you ever think you'd get to meet the king of Southwestern outlaws in the flesh? This is a genuine special occasion for us."

Ki reached out and shook Lomax's hand as Jessie had just done. "When we came upon your little dispute here, we thought we were helping out some two-bit outfit that had maybe raised a little too much ruckus to suit the law in some border town. We had no idea we were coming to the aid of Bud Lomax himself."

He lies like a politician, Jessie thought to herself, suppressing a smile. Better even than I do.

"I'm obliged to the pair of you," Lomax said, "for your help."

"We'd best get going if we're to get to the ranch before dark," Standish interjected. "Colfax has been hit in the arm and needs patching up."

"How about you two?" Lomax asked Jessie and Ki. "Would you consider joining my outfit? We could use a couple of crack shots such as yourselves."

"We work alone," Jessie declared.

Ki avoided looking at her as he wondered why she was turning down—she *was* turning down Lomax's offer, wasn't she?—when the whole object of their having joined the

72

gunfight with the Rangers was to achieve what Lomax was now offering—a chance to join his gang and maybe recover the Firebird from him.

"You'd get a fair share of the loot we take in," Lomax offered.

"When we rob trains or people or banks," Jessie said, "we split the loot just *two* ways."

"Penny-ante stuff, no doubt," Lomax said derisively. "You two can't operate on the scale that a gang like mine can—and damn well does. Why, we've taken whole herds of cattle from drovers working for outfits like Charlie Goodnight's and sold them off and split the cash amongst ourselves. You couldn't hope to mount an operation that big."

Jessie glanced at Ki. "He's right. What do you say? Do you want to throw in with Lomax?"

Playing Jessie's hard-to-get game, Ki stroked his chin and said, "I kind of like the way things are right now, Jessie." Which, he thought, was the truth—on one level, at least.

Jessie argued with him, with the result that Ki finally appeared to give in to her.

"Okay," he said, "we'll join Lomax's outfit."

"Good," Jessie said.

"But if I don't like it once we're in, I'm riding out. No long-term commitments for me. As long as that's understood, I'm in."

"Let's ride," Lomax said.

Chapter 5

The sun, a bright red ball in an orange sky, was setting when they came within sight of the ranch, which was located in a shallow valley surrounded by low hills.

"That's where we hang our hats," Lomax announced as they rode toward it. "Don't know whose place it was to start with. We came upon it in this out-of-the-way spot a while back, and it was empty, so we decided it was a good enough spot to work out of."

As they rode from the crest of one of the hills down into the valley, Jessie caught a glimpse of what she thought was a woman in the ranch's doorway. But when she looked more closely, she saw that the doorway was empty. A trick of the sun's dying light, she decided.

Lomax, Jessie and Ki dismounted in front of the house while Standish and the rest of the gang members made their way to the bunkhouse behind it.

Once inside, Lomax went to the cast-iron stove and stirred something in a huge pot that sat on it. He tasted the pot's contents, smacked his lips and said, "Beef stew. Courtesy of one of Charlie Goodnight's steers we kept for ourselves instead of selling it off like we did the rest. Did I tell you about us rustling old Charlie's herd on the Goodnight-Loving Trail?"

"You did," Jessie said.

"Where do you sell the cattle you steal?" Ki inquired.

"After we brand-blot them and write ourselves a forged bill of sale, we unload them up over the line in Indian Territory as a rule. Those Chickasaws up that way, they don't ask a whole lot of questions about the whys and wherefores of the beef we've got to sell. They're too busy getting rich to worry about how they get that way.

"You two hungry?" Lomax asked as he spooned some stew onto a tin plate for himself. "If you are, help yourselves. There's plenty."

Jessie went to the stove, took down two plates from a shelf above it and spooned stew onto them. She gave one to Ki and sat down with the remaining one across the table from Lomax, who was busily—and noisily—eating.

"There's bread in the box," he muttered.

Ki opened the bread box and took out half a loaf of bread. Seeing no knife, he broke off a piece and set the remainder of the loaf in the center of the table.

As she ate, Jessie surveyed the room. There was an iron safe in one corner. Its door was shut and, she assumed, locked. There was a door on the far side of the large room, which led, she supposed, to the sleeping quarters.

"You can stay in one of the bedrooms in here," Lomax told her. "Ki, you'll bunk out back with the rest of the boys."

Jessie cleaned her plate and then announced that she wanted to get some things from her saddlebag. As she made her way to the door, Lomax said, "Your friend can unsaddle our horses and put them in the corral for the night."

Ki rose and followed Jessie outside. "What are you up to?" he asked her once they were in no danger of being overheard by Lomax. "You haven't got anything in your saddlebag."

"That remark of mine was just an excuse to come out here and go through Lomax's saddlebags in case he's got my brooch in one of them, although I admit that's an unlikely possibility."

As Ki unsaddled Lomax's horse, Jessie rooted through the gang leader's saddlebags. Her brooch was in neither of them.

"He must have it on him," Ki said, "if he still has it."

Jessie nodded and then returned to the ranch.

"I thought you wanted to get something from your saddle-bag," Lomax said as she rejoined him, leaning back on the rear legs of his chair, his boots propped up on the chair's front rung.

"Uh . . . yes, I did," Jessie said, realizing that he had almost caught her out. She pulled a small comb from her pocket and held it up.

" 'Vanity of vanities,' saith the preacher, 'all is vanity,' " Lomax quoted with a lopsided grin. He brought his chair down to the floor with a resounding crack, rose and walked around the table to where Jessie was standing. Without pre-amble, he seized her by the shoulders and roughly kissed her.

She managed to shove him away, resisting the impulse to wipe the sour taste of him from her mouth with the back of her hand.

"I'm tired," she said. "Ki and I were on the trail since before dawn this morning. I'd like to bed down now if that's all right with you."

"Anybody else," a disgruntled Lomax muttered, "would have insisted that you sing—that is to say, fuck—for your supper, Jessie. But not me. When one door closes, anoth-er one opens up. You take the room at the end of the hall."

Jessie watched Lomax turn and leave the room. Then she rose and made her way to the room at the end of the hall that Lomax had assigned her. She found it to be both dirty and odorous. There were no sheets or blankets on the bed, only

76

a stained mattress leaking some of its straw from a gaping hole. Dust covered the room's furniture. A pair of men's boots, one of them missing a heel, lay on the floor.

Jessie went to the room's single window and opened it in an effort to dispel the pungent odors and then sat down on the edge of the bed, trying to decide on her next move. When she heard a noise in the hall, she rose, went to the door and peered out.

A naked Lomax left the room next door and padded bare-footed down the hall toward the main room of the house, his hefty buttocks swiveling.

Jessie hesitated only momentarily. Then, when Lomax had exited the hall, she made a dash down it and darted into the room he had just left. She went to where his clothes lay, some of them on the floor and some of them draped over a listing cane-backed chair, and began to search through his pockets. She could hear voices—Lomax's and a woman's—coming from the main room. She could make out only a few words of the conversation taking place between the pair.

Lomax: "Where . . . you been?"

The woman: " . . . bunkhouse . . . cooking."

She thrust a hand into each of Lomax's boots and found nothing hidden in either of them. Neither was her brooch concealed in the rolled-up cuffs of his trousers or in his leather hatband. She started at the sound of a metallic clang that had just come from the main room. She hurriedly searched the drawers of a bureau and found nothing in them but a few Mexican pesos and a woman's soiled underwear.

She was heading for the door on her way back to her own room when she heard footsteps outside in the hall. Footsteps and the voices of Lomax and the unknown woman. Frantic at the possibility of discovery, she started for the window, intending to climb through it. But it was too late for that, she realized. The voices and footsteps were now right outside the door of the room. She took refuge behind a ragged cloth hanging from a crossbar, a space that apparently served as a closet and storeroom. It was filled with empty bags and boxes, which she almost tripped over in her haste.

"Did you miss me, Polly, my sweet pussy?" Lomax asked as he shoved a disheveled woman into his room and then followed her inside.

Through one of several of the rents in the cloth covering her hiding place, Jessie recognized the woman as the one she had caught a brief glimpse of as she rode toward the ranch earlier. The woman looked worn and pale. Her brown hair hung in strings over her forehead and down her neck despite her efforts to pin it up. There were smudges of dirt on her pretty, somewhat childlike face. She stood with her back and the palms of her hands pressed against the wall. Her eyes were fastened on Lomax, who stood facing her, his hands on his hips, his manhood rampant.

"Did you miss this, Polly?" he asked, gripping his massive erection in his right hand and waving it lewdly at her. "It missed you."

When Polly made no reply, Lomax frowned. "I asked you a question, dammit! Answer it!"

"N-no—I mean, yes, I missed you, Bud."

Lomax's frown faded. He almost smiled. "And this?" He aimed his tumescent rod at her.

She nodded.

"Speak up, woman!"

"I missed that too, Bud."

"I'll bet you did. This one beats your husband's by a country mile, doesn't it, pretty Polly?"

She nodded again.

"Clarence Jessup wouldn't know how to take care of a hot and hearty woman like yourself if he spent years studying up on the subject. But Bud Lomax, he knows how to satisfy you. Am I right, Mrs. Clarence Jessup?"

Polly raised a fisted hand and placed it over her mouth to try to stifle a sob that nevertheless escaped her lips. Two tears slid down her cheeks.

"Turn off the damned waterworks, woman!" Lomax bellowed at her.

She shuddered and seemed to be trying to melt into the solid wall behind her.

Lomax took a step toward her. "Show me how glad you are to see me home, honey."

Polly's fist slowly left her lips. As slowly, her arms went around Lomax's neck. She kissed him on the lips, her eyes squeezed shut.

"Aahhh," he sighed, grinning. "Now give that thing down there a welcome home."

Polly's right hand slid down along Lomax's curly-haired chest, across the slightly mounded expanse of his equally hairy belly, and entered the forest of his pubic hair. Then her hand encircled his shaft. She squeezed it, her eyes open once again and staring dully at the opposite wall.

"Stroke it," Lomax ordered.

Polly obediently did.

From her hiding place, Jessie continued to watch, hoping for an opportunity to slip unnoticed from the room, terrified that she was going to sneeze at any moment because of the thick dust in the air of the space she occupied.

"That was one sweet kiss you gave me just now, Polly," Lomax said. "You got one just like it for what you've got in your hot little hand?"

A sigh that was more of a moan slid from between Polly's lips. A resigned expression stiffened the delicate features of her face as her knees began to bend and her body folded down upon itself until she was kneeling in front of the naked Lomax.

As his hands returned to his hips, she gripped his shaft in both hands and kissed its head. When she withdrew her lips, it glistened.

79

"Take off your clothes and get on the bed," Lomax ordered.

Polly disrobed and got on the bed.

"Turn over."

"No, Bud, please. Not like that. It hurts when you do that to me."

Lomax struck her with his open hand, the blow leaving a red mark on her cheek.

She began to cry.

He raised his hand, prepared to strike again.

She stopped crying and turned over on her stomach.

Lomax climbed onto the bed, spread her legs and mounted her from behind.

Polly let out an anguished cry as he penetrated her anally.

Lomax paid no attention to her. He grunted, reached down, gripped his shaft, and forced it all the way into her. Then he began to buck, slowly at first, and then more rapidly. His grunts resounded in the room and blended with Polly's strangled weeping. Soon he was sweating as a result of his lusty efforts. His wet body slapped against Polly's. His thrusting continued without interruption for several minutes. Then he began to breathe heavily, his lips parted, his eyes shut. He deliberately slowed his movement to postpone his climax.

"Do like I taught you to do," he muttered between clenched teeth. "Don't just lie there like a bump on a goddamned log, for Christ's sweet sake!"

Polly thrust her buttocks up to meet him. She began to move them in a way that matched Lomax's rhythm—up, down, up, down again.

He let out a wordless cry that became a wail and threw his head back. He seized Polly's buttocks in both hands and held them against him as his pelvis jerked, shuddered, jerked again and he filled her with his seed.

"Good," he murmured after a long moment when they

seemed locked together, never to part. "You're getting better at what I've been teaching you to do," he added as he pulled out of Polly. Flopping down on his back on the bed, he clasped his hands behind his head and said, "Maybe I'll give you a reward for good behavior."

Polly lay motionless with her head twisted away from him. She made no response to his remark.

"I picked up something real special this time out."

Still Polly said nothing.

"Talk to me, bitch!" he demanded, reaching out and slapping her smartly on the rump.

"What?" she responded. "What did you pick up, Bud?"

"A brooch," he told her, once again clasping his hands behind his head and staring up at the ceiling. "A really nice brooch. A *ruby* brooch. What do you think of that?"

"That's nice."

"That's nice? Is that all you can say? Why, hell, that brooch is worth ten times its weight in gold. Maybe even more."

"Is it for me?" A question spoken in a voice without hope.

"Maybe it is. Maybe it is for you, who knows? If you keep on being nice to me—who knows? But for now it stays in the safe where I put it just before you sashayed into the house."

In her hiding place, Jessie's heart leaped. She remained where she was, excited by the knowledge that the brooch was so close. And yet so far, locked as it was in an iron safe to which she did not know the combination. But she would get her hands on the Firebird. Somehow she would, she silently vowed.

Beyond the ragged cloth that hid her from the two people on the bed, Lomax had fallen asleep and was loudly snoring. Jessie watched without moving a muscle as Polly climbed wearily and somewhat painfully out of the bed, picked up her clothes and, dragging them listlessly along the floor behind her, left the room.

Jessie waited several minutes and then slipped out of the room and into her own without being observed by anyone.

Jessie awoke the next morning to the smell of salt pork frying, which permeated her bedroom despite the fact that the door was closed. By the time she had washed and dressed, the smell had grown stronger. She could hear voices coming from the main room of the house. When she entered it a few minutes later, she found Lomax and Polly there. Polly at the stove, Lomax seated at the table.

"Have a seat," Lomax said to her, gesturing to an empty chair next to him.

Jessie took the one opposite him instead.

"What'll you have, Jessie?" he asked. "Just tell the chief cook and bottle washer, and she'll see to it that you get it."

Polly glanced in Jessie's direction.

"Anything you have," Jessie said to her, "will be fine with me."

Within minutes, Polly placed a plate containing salt pork and boiled beans before her. She poured coffee into a tin cup and placed it beside Jessie's plate.

Lomax, rubbing his gut with both hands, rose and announced, "See you later, Jessie. Me and the boys are going into Laredo this morning. They got themselves a bunch of banks in Laredo, and we aim to rob them all one by one."

When Lomax had gone, Jessie proceeded to devour her breakfast, surprised at how hungry she was.

"More coffee?" Polly asked her when she emptied her cup.

"Yes, please. Another cup would be welcome."

Polly poured it and started to leave the room.

"Don't go."

Polly, at the door, turned. "I've got to clean the bunkhouse."

"Right now?"

Polly hesitated, one hand on the door's knob. "Is there something you want?"

"Just to talk. Sit down, why don't you?"

When Jessie pulled out a chair, Polly hesitated and then crossed the room and sat down on it.

"My name's Jessie. I just met Lomax yesterday. Have you known him long?"

Polly looked away, unable to meet Jessie's inquiring gaze.

"You keep house for him, I gather."

Polly lowered her head. Nodded. Began to weep softly.

Jessie reached out and touched her hands, which were folded in front of her on top of the table. "What is it? What's wrong, Polly?"

The woman's tears flowed. Jessie simply sat beside her, touching her hands, waiting for the emotional storm to pass.

When it finally did, Polly sniffed several times and then, speaking in a harsh tone, said, "I hate him. I hate that man with a most unholy passion."

"Lomax?"

"I wish I could kill him. But I don't have the nerve."

"Why would you want to kill him?"

"He kidnapped me. It happened weeks ago—nearly a month ago now. He took me away from my home and husband. His name's Clarence Jessup. He's a lawyer. A very respected man in the community. In fact, he is planning on running for governor on the Republican ticket."

"How did it happen—the kidnapping?"

"I was in the bank. Bud and his boys burst in and robbed it. On the way out, as they were leaving, Bud spotted me. He came over to me, grabbed me by the wrist, dragged me screaming out of the bank, put me on his horse and rode away with me. He never said a word. He just did it. But that's Bud. He sees something he fancies, he takes it."

Jessie thought of the Firebird.

"Takes it and uses it," Polly added morosely.

"Hasn't anyone come looking for you?"

"Not that I know of. I'm not all that sure that Clarence would want that to happen."

"Not want it to happen? Why ever not?"

"If everyone throughout the state of Texas came to know about Clarence's wife having been carted off by the notorious Bud Lomax, it would cause a scandal the likes of which would be sure to seriously injure Clarence's political prospects. Even if Clarence had sent men to search for me— if they found me, I would be damaged goods, if you take my meaning. Clarence's future would be seriously jeopardized."

Anger surged within Jessie as an image of what she had witnessed the night before in Lomax's bedroom blazed in her memory—an image of Polly being forced to kneel and kiss . . .

She said, "What about *your* future?"

"I suppose it's here—with Bud."

"You haven't tried to escape?"

"Where would I go?"

"Home, that's where. Home to your husband."

"Oh, I couldn't do that."

"Why not, for heaven's sake?"

"I told you—Clarence has a bright future in politics. For now, that future is on a state level. But who knows. In time he could be running for national office. Perhaps even for the presidency. I would be a hindrance to him as a result of all that has happened to me here. Then, too, if I were to leave here—Bud has threatened to kill me if I do. He said he would also kill Clarence. I couldn't let that happen. I just couldn't be responsible for anything bad happening to Clarence."

"The two of you could go away together," Jessie suggested. "Someplace where Lomax wouldn't be able to find you. You could start a whole new life together. Leave the past behind you."

"That would take money. A great deal of money. It would take time for Clarence to become established in his profession in a new place."

"He loves you, doesn't he?" Jessie asked.

"Oh, yes."

"And you love him?"

"More than I can say."

"Then together you could do it. You know what they say: 'Love conquers all.' "

"Do you really think it would work?"

"I'm sure it would. Whatever problems you two might have as a result of Lomax having abducted you, I'm sure they can be worked out. You have love on your side."

For the first time since Jessie had first seen her, Polly smiled. Then her smile gave way to a frown.

"I'm not sure I'd dare do it. If I ran off, Bud would come after me. He might catch me, and if he did, I hate to think what he would do to me for running away from him."

"I'm not saying that would not be a problem. It well might be. But what you've got to do, Polly, is think of what is to be gained by getting away from here and him as opposed to what will happen if you remain here out of fear of him."

Polly's lips twisted in an unmistakable expression of distaste. Rising, she started for the door. "I'll think about it," she said before heading down the hall.

Jessie rose and left the house. She made her way to the bunkhouse, which she found deserted except for Ki, who was pouring himself a cup of coffee from a pot that sat on a stove in the middle of the rectangular room.

"Good morning, Jessie. I was just about to head for the house to see how you were doing."

"Ki, I know where the Firebird is."

He carefully put down his cup and stared at Jessie. "You know where it is?"

"It's in that safe in the house. Did you notice the safe?"

85

"I noticed it. It might as well be on the moon, your brooch."

"What—"

"How are we going to get it out of the safe?"

"We'll find a way."

"You've got some nitroglycerine to blow it open with?"

"Don't make jokes. This is serious business."

"I know it is."

"Maybe we can find the combination that will unlock the safe. I remember one time when I was a child and our safe at home was robbed. I remember my father talking about the incident after the man who had robbed us had been caught and jailed. The man bragged to the marshal about how he had gotten into the safe. It was easy, he claimed. Most people, he said, choose combinations for their safes that are easy to remember and usually, therefore, quite simple. My father, for example, used four numbers he found easy to remember—two, four, six and eight in that order. The thief said he tried such numerical combinations which had worked for him in the past as he tried to unlock our safe. It was time-consuming, I gather, but it paid off for him in the end when he hit upon my father's combination. He also said, as I recall, that people often used their date of birth for a safe's combination. The number of the month—five, say, for May. Then the number or numbers for the date followed by four digits for the year."

"We don't know Lomax's date of birth, and I'm no whiz at numerology."

"We've got to try," Jessie insisted somewhat impatiently.

"You're right about that. Nothing ventured, nothing gained. By the way, how did you find out that your brooch is in the safe?"

"Polly Jessup told me."

"Is that the woman who was cooking in the bunkhouse last night after we arrived?" When Jessie nodded, Ki asked, "Is she Lomax's mistress?"

"In a manner of speaking, yes." Jessie proceeded to discreetly describe what she had inadvertently witnessed and overheard during the encounter between Lomax and Polly the previous night. Then she recounted her conversation with Polly after Lomax had left the ranch.

"She's got herself into a pretty bad situation, it appears," Ki commented. "I hope she can find the courage to get herself out of it."

"So do I. Now let's go back to the house and try to open the safe."

"What if she catches us at it?"

"Polly? I'm afraid I hadn't given that possibility a thought. Tell you what. You have a way with women, as I've noticed on occasions in the past. You go find Polly and distract her while I try to open the safe."

Laughing together, they hurried back to the house. Once inside, Jessie pointed to the hall and said, "Just before I left the house, Polly went down there."

Ki gave her a smart salute and started down the hall. As he did so, Jessie went to the safe and knelt down in front of it. She began to go through the multiplication tables, starting with the twos. She was on the fours when Ki returned and announced, "Polly's not here. That is to say she's not in any of the bedrooms."

Jessie, intent on what she was doing, barely heard him; nor did she notice when he left the house. By the time Ki returned she had gone completely through the multiplication tables with the frustrating result that the safe remained stubbornly locked.

"I see you haven't hit on the combination," Ki observed. "Any more than I've been able to find Polly. She seems to have vanished into thin air. I even looked down the well. No Polly."

Jessie clenched her fists. "We might have to take a sledge to this thing to open it."

"I could ride into Laredo and buy some dynamite."

Jessie shook her head. "We ought to be able to find the combination. It can't be anything too complicated. Lomax doesn't strike me as the kind of man who would go for anything very complex. He'd want a combination that he could easily keep in mind. Do you want to have a try at opening this thing?"

Ki replaced Jessie in front of the safe. He sat cross-legged on the floor staring at the dial, trying to come up with the right combination of numbers. He began to turn the dial randomly. To the right, to the left . . .

Nothing worked. Nothing, that is, until he tried turning the dial to number one on the right, number two on the left, number three on the right—and so on until he reached the number eight.

The safe's tumblers clicked, sounding loud in the otherwise quiet room.

Ki looked up at Jessie, who was staring at the safe. Then he gripped the safe's handle, twisted it—and the iron door swung open.

"You did it!" a gleeful Jessie cried, dropping down on her knees next to him.

"Damned if I didn't," he said, surprised at his success.

"*How* did you do it?"

"I used Lomax's name. 'Bud Lomax' has eight letters in it. I used the numbers one to eight in sequence. Simple as pie when you come to think about it."

Jessie's face fell. "There's nothing inside the safe."

Ki peered into it and saw that she was right. "I thought you were sure the Firebird was inside here."

"I was sure. As I told you, I heard Lomax say so to Polly when they were in bed together."

"Maybe he lied."

"But why would he?"

"Beats me."

Jessie slumped down on the floor as she stared disconsolately into the empty safe. "I saw him walking down the hall without a stitch of clothes on. I went into his bedroom and searched through his clothes. My brooch wasn't there. He came back into the room with Polly after only a few moments. I even heard the sound of metal striking metal only a moment before he returned. Now that I think about it, what I heard must have been the sound of the safe door being closed after he had placed the Firebird in the safe."

"Then where is it?"

Ki's question triggered a thought in Jessie's mind and made her ask one of her own. "Where is Polly Jessup?"

They both stared at one another for a moment and then Ki said, "You think she took the brooch?"

"She must have. It's the only explanation I can think of for it being missing."

"I can think of another one. Maybe Lomax took it out of the safe before you woke up this morning, with the intention of disposing of it."

"Oh, no!"

Jessie and Ki were impatiently waiting for him when Lomax returned several hours later.

He had no sooner entered the house when he looked at the stove and said, "I'm starving. Where the hell's Polly? Why hasn't she got supper cooking?"

"We haven't seen her for hours," Jessie said. "Not since shortly after you and your boys left for Laredo. By the way, did you check out the banks as you said you were going to do?"

Lomax grinned and tossed on the table some folding money he had taken from his pocket. "We checked them out. We're going to hit the Farmers' Federal when it opens first thing tomorrow morning. Then we'll have a lot more money to add to that measly pile there. The cost of supplies is shooting through the roof. I bought what we needed in town today, and the buying just about bankrupted me."

Lomax sat down and began to count the money on the

table, wetting his thumb in order to do so easily.

"The Farmers' Federal," he said, "has one teller who also happens to be the owner of the outfit. We asked around and found out that his bank handles the payroll for the Bent B ranch outside of town. That, folks told us, is a hefty sum. The Bent B has nineteen hired hands and a cook, and tomorrow's the end of the month, which means it's payday. So, Jessie, you and Ki get a good night's sleep tonight. We'll be heading back to Laredo and the Farmers' Federal at first light."

Moments later, when Lomax finished counting the money, he rose and went to the safe, the door of which Ki had closed before the man's return. He bent down and proceeded to turn the dial first to the right, then to the left . . .

When he had opened the safe, he carelessly tossed the money he had been counting onto a shelf. He had no sooner done so than he let out a lusty epithet. Which was promptly followed by, "It's gone! The damned thing is gone!"

"What's gone?" Jessie asked innocently.

"There was a piece of jewelry in here this morning when I took out the money I'd need for supplies. It was a woman's ruby brooch and it was a beauty. Worth a fortune too." Lomax rose. He turned to face Jessie and Ki. "You didn't by any chance take it, did you?"

"How could we take it?" Ki indignantly asked. "We don't know the combination to that safe of yours," he lied glibly.

"If we had taken it," Jessie said, "and it was worth the fortune you said it was, we'd have been long gone from here with it by now."

Lomax was considering their remarks when one of his men entered the house.

"Boss, that Appaloosa in your string—"

"Adams, search those two."

"What?"

"I said search them," Lomax repeated. "See if you can find a ruby brooch on either one of them."

Adams, with a sceptical glance at Lomax, ordered Jessie and Ki to stand up. When they had done so, he searched them, blushing as he patted Jessie down and thrust his hands into her pockets.

"They're clean, Boss," he said when he had finished his search. "Neither one of them has any kind of a brooch on them."

Lomax's eyes narrowed. "Polly!" he roared. When he received no reply to his shouted summons, he turned to Adams. "Have you seen that slut since we got back?"

"No, Boss, I've not."

"She took it," Lomax said. "I'll bet my bottom dollar on it. I told her about the brooch last night. I told her I might even give it to her, which I never had any intention of doing. Somehow or other she got into the safe and made off with it."

"How could she have done that?" Ki asked. "Did she know the combination?"

Lomax hesitated a moment. Then, "No, she didn't. I mean I don't think she knew it. But wait a minute. She's been in here cooking and cleaning and doing one thing and another plenty of times when I've opened that safe. She could have watched me and seen the combination and remembered it. That must be it. She must have finally gotten up enough gumption to rob me and run."

"Maybe that's got something to do with your Appaloosa I come here about," Adams offered.

"What the hell are you talking about?" Lomax barked.

"I came here to tell you that your Appaloosa isn't in the corral, Boss. He's no fence jumper, so I figured somebody must have stole him while we were in town today."

Muttering obscenities, Lomax left the room. He returned a few minutes later and announced, "My extra saddle's gone too. That clinches it. Polly got in the safe, took the brooch and my horse and saddle and made off with the whole kit and caboodle."

"What are you going to do, Boss?" Adams asked as Lomax headed for the door.

"What the hell do you think I'm going to do? I'm going after her."

When Lomax had stormed out of the house followed by Adams, Ki said to Jessie, "We could trail Lomax."

"I've got a better idea. Come on."

Ki followed her out of the house, where they found Lomax swinging into the saddle.

"We'll go with you," Jessie said, "just in case you run into any trouble."

Lomax, in the saddle, looked down at them. "You don't think I can handle Polly alone?"

"I've no doubt you can," Jessie said smoothly. "But it can't hurt you to have us along in case something goes wrong. If that brooch you think Polly stole from you is as valuable as you say it is, she's not liable to give it up without a fight."

"Maybe you're right. It can't hurt, like you said, to have you two siding me. Let's go."

Chapter 6

"Where do you think she is?" Ki asked Lomax as they all rode down from the crest of a hill an hour later.

"That's easy to answer. I found her in a fair-sized town called Elmont due west of here. She had a husband, she told me. Where the hell else would she go but back to him?"

"She might have decided to strike out on her own," Jessie ventured.

"Not likely. Not Polly Jessup. She's not the independent sort. She's the kind of woman can't do without there's a man around she can run to in time of trouble."

They rode on in silence for a time, a silence that was finally broken by Ki, who commented, "There's smoke on the horizon up ahead."

"That'd be Elmont," Lomax said and spurred his horse.

Ki and Jessie did the same in order to keep up with him.

Minutes later, they were riding into Elmont, a town that sprawled on the prairie like an ever-growing organism. Lengths of board were piled on empty lots, ready to be transformed into dwellings. A boardwalk fronting a row of shops was under construction. Hammers pounded nails and saws bit into wood throughout the town, adding their voices to the general hubbub.

"See that bank over there," Lomax said, nodding to a one-story building with a barred front window. "That's where Polly and me first met. She was in there on business and so were me and my boys. *We* were there to rob the place and that's just what we did. Finding Polly and taking her back to the ranch with me was an extra bonus I found that day."

Lomax laughed, the sound a rumbling in his throat. "Hey, you!" he yelled to a man who was lounging in front of a tin shop. "Where's the Jessup place?"

"You talking about Clarence Jessup, the lawyer fella?" the man yelled back.

"I am if he's got himself a wife called Polly."

The man pointed to a side street. "He's got an office right around the corner there on Mulberry Street, and he's got a house in the middle of Clay Street. Number twelve, it is."

Lomax spurred his horse into a trot and rode on without bothering to thank his informant.

"We've passed Mulberry Street," Jessie pointed out to him.

"I don't think she'd be in her husband's office," Lomax said. "More likely, she's to home. We'll try there first."

When they reached number twelve Clay Street, they found themselves in front of a neat frame house painted white with black shutters flanking all the sparkling windows. A white picket fence surrounded the property, where yellow marigolds were in bloom.

Lomax dismounted, went through the gate in the fence and up to the front door of the house. He tried the door and, finding it locked, stepped backward, raised one booted foot and slammed it into the door.

The door shattered and swung inward, trailing splintered wood.

Jessie, as she dismounted and Ki did the same, expected Polly, if she were inside the house, to scream at the sudden invasion of her home. No scream came. Jessie ran toward the house with Ki by her side as Lomax disappeared into it.

94

When she burst into the house she found Lomax confronting a tall, thin man whose gray eyes gleamed behind his spectacles and whose dun-colored hair was parted neatly in the middle.

"What is the meaning of this, sir?" the man asked indignantly, his pale face reddening. "How dare you burst into my home like this and—"

"Shut up, Jessup!" Lomax snarled. "You are Jessup, I take it?"

"I am Clarence Jessup, yes. Who, sir, are you?"

"Never you mind who I am. Where's your wife?"

Jessup's face assumed a mournful expression. "My wife is not here. The unfortunate woman was abducted some weeks ago by a gang of outlaws. I have not seen or heard a word from her since that sad day. But what right have you to ask me questions, to invade my home, to destroy my privacy—"

"Don't make me any lists, Jessup," Lomax interrupted. "I've got no use for lists, least of all those that catalog all my many faults and shortcomings. For your information, I happen to be the man who took your wife away from you."

"Why, you scurrilous—"

"There you go again, Jessup, adding on to your list." Lomax drew his gun, causing Jessup to shrink from him and raise his hands in a futile gesture of self-defense.

"Your wife ran off from me today, Jessup. She stole a horse I prize. She also stole something else I prize even more. I'm here to get back from her what belongs to me. I *intend* to get it back, by hook or by crook. Now, I think you're lying through your pearly white teeth to me, Jessup. I think you know where your wife is. I think she came hightailing it right here to you after she left me. Where is she, Jessup?"

The lawyer shook his head, tried to speak, couldn't.

"Do I have to shoot you to make you talk to me, Jessup?" Lomax persisted, thumbing back the hammer of the gun in his hand.

"I don't know what you're talking about," Jessup managed to blurt out. "I mean I know what you said and I understand it, but about Polly—I don't know where she is, so help me, God, I don't!"

"If she didn't come here when she left me, where do you think she might have headed instead?"

"I really couldn't say. She has no kinfolks in this area. Her family is back east. In Rochester, New York."

"Hold your gun on him," Lomax ordered Jessie. "Me and Ki, we'll search the house."

"No!" Jessup cried, shaking his head from side to side so vigorously that his hair flew about his face. "I won't let you search my house. You have absolutely no right—"

Lomax calmly fired a shot that bit into the board floor directly in front of Jessup's feet.

The lawyer's mouth snapped shut. His eyes were wild with fear as he stared at the smoke curling up from the barrel of Lomax's revolver.

After nodding to Jessie and beckoning to Ki, Lomax made his way out of the room, Ki right behind him.

"This is terrible," Jessup whispered in a shaky voice. "I have never had any dealings with outlaws before. Now both my wife and I have fallen into their clutches. Are you going to shoot me?"

"No, Mr. Jessup, I'm not," Jessie answered. "Not if you're telling us the truth, that is."

"Oh, I am, I most definitely am telling you the truth. I swear to you that I am."

"If you're lying—if we do find your wife hiding somewhere here in the house—*I* won't shoot you, but my partner, Lomax, will probably do so."

Jessup blanched, "I have to use the outhouse. I'm afraid I'm going to—"

"Stay put, Mr. Jessup," Jessie ordered as the sounds reached her ears of Lomax and Ki searching the other rooms of the house.

Later, when both men returned and had searched the one remaining room, which Jessie and Jessup occupied, Lomax announced, "She's not here."

"We couldn't find her," Ki declared.

Jessie didn't fail to notice the subtle difference in the two statements. Lomax had unequivocally concluded that Polly Jessup was not in the house. But Ki, on the other hand, had left open the possibility that she might indeed be present but as yet unfound.

"Jessup," Lomax growled, "I'm going to find your wife and—"

"I want her back," Jessup wailed, his eyes beginning to glisten.

"You'll get her back, but maybe you won't want her back by the time I'm through with the thieving little bitch."

Jessie and Ki followed Lomax as he stormed out of the house.

As they swung into their saddles, Lomax muttered, "Where the hell can she be?" talking more to himself that to either of his companions.

But Jessie responded to his question. "We could check at the livery barn."

"For what?" a disgruntled Lomax asked as he wheeled his horse and started down the street.

"The livery barn is something like a telegraph office," Jessie stated as she rode alongside him. Ignoring the skeptical look on his face, she added, "It's a place where information comes in and goes out all day long. Strangers come to town and board their horses there. Before long the whole town knows who the stranger is and where he came from and what his business is. People leave messages for one another there. The men who loiter at such places—the livery barn bums, as some people call them—they have their fingers on the pulse of a town."

"I agree with Jessie," Ki stated, "but before we try the livery barn or the saloons for word of Polly, I suggest we check Jessup's law office. It strikes me as rather strange that a businessman such as himself would be home at this time of day. Maybe we'll find an explanation for his absence from his office at his office."

"He probably just went home for dinner," Lomax grumbled.

"Maybe," Ki said, "but I'm inclined to doubt that. A bachelor—and Jessup's been a bachelor, in effect, since you abducted his wife—he'd be more inclined, I think, to go to a restaurant rather than try to prepare a meal for himself."

"Ki has a point," Jessie said. "Most bachelors I know would starve to death if they had to cook their own meals. I've yet to meet one who knows much more about the culinary arts than how to boil water."

When Lomax made no objection, the three headed for the law office of Clarence Jessup. They left their mounts at the hitchrail in front of the building and went inside.

"Good day," a clerk wearing a green eyeshade greeted them. "May I be of service?"

"Where—" Lomax began but was silenced by Jessie, who held up a hand.

"We're looking for Mrs. Jessup," she told the clerk. "Is she here?"

"My, oh, my," exclaimed the clerk, breaking into a broad smile. "News certainly does travel fast, doesn't it?"

"Then she's here?" Jessie asked, barely suppressing the excitement she was beginning to feel.

"Oh, my, no. Mrs. Jessup went home with her husband just minutes after she arrived here in the office earlier today. She was all excited and could hardly put one word in front of another so Mr. Jessup just ushered her out of the office after telling me he was taking her home. I do hope they have a pleasant reunion. It was a terrible thing, poor Mrs. Jessup being snatched away like that by a ruthless gang of outlaws. But since she's come back now I guess one can only observe that all's well that ends well."

Lomax opened his mouth to say something, but Jessie prevented him from speaking by seizing his elbow and quickly escorting him out of the office.

Once outside, she said, "Polly must be somewhere in the Jessup house."

"She couldn't be," Lomax argued. "Ki and me, we searched every inch of it. We looked under every bed, in every closet—"

"There might be someplace we overlooked," Ki pointed out.

"Did you leave the house while we were there?" Jessie suddenly asked excitedly as a thought occurred to her.

"No, why would we?" Lomax answered.

"Clarence Jessup wasn't at all happy about you wanting to search the premises," Jessie mused. "I don't think he would have been that upset about a search unless—"

"He had something to hide," Ki said, finishing Jessie's sentence for her, as each of them often did for the other because of their keen awareness of each other's thought processes.

"Exactly," Jessie said, nodding. "Something to hide by the name of Polly Jessup, devoted wife and helpmate of Clarence."

As they boarded their horses and started back the way they had come, Jessie said, "I don't think we'll find Polly in the house though."

Lomax shot her a disbelieving look. "Then what's this all about Jessup hiding his wife someplace so that we couldn't find her when we looked for her?"

Jessie's only answer was a small secret smile.

When they arrived for the second time at the Jessup house on Clay Street, Lomax slid out of the saddle before his horse had stopped moving and strode briskly up to the broken front door. "Jessup!" he yelled as he entered the house and again, "Jessup!"

By the time Jessie and Ki had joined him, he was raging

back and forth from one room to the next, up the stairs to the second floor and then back down again.

"Now it's *him* that's not here!" he bellowed, kicking an overstuffed hassock out of his way with such force that it went careening into a table next to the fireplace and knocked it over. "Now they're *both* not here!"

Jessie, annoyed by the man's display of childlike petulance, went past him and into the kitchen at the rear of the house. She went outside, letting the screen door slam behind her, and climbed the low rise to where the outhouse stood, a silent and solitary sentinel.

Ki, who had followed her outside, stopped when he saw where she was headed. He was about to turn and reenter the house, where Lomax was volubly raging, when Jessie called his name.

He sprinted up the grade to the open door of the outhouse and halted when he spotted Jessie kneeling on the dirt floor inside the malodorous structure, beside the crumpled body of Polly Jessup. He stood there staring at the blood on Polly's forehead, which had drawn flies, the perennial tenants of such buildings as the one she was so forlornly lying in.

"She's hurt badly," Jessie said without looking up at Ki as she eased Polly's left arm out from under her body, where it had been imprisoned.

"Is she conscious?"

"Yes, I think so. Polly?" When she received no answer, Jessie said, "Can you hear me, Polly?"

The prone figure seemed to stiffen. Polly's eyes quivered, startling a cluster of flies that had been feeding on the blood seeping from the deep wound on her forehead.

"Polly?" Jessie repeated.

Her eyes flickered. One opened halfway and stared dully up at Jessie.

"Can you talk?" Jessie asked her. "Can you tell me what happened to you?"

"Clarence . . . " Polly's voice was barely audible. "He hit—hurt—me. He said . . . I should have tried to escape. He said—" Tears oozed out of Polly's eyes, both the one that was open and the still-closed one. After a moment she said, "He doesn't want anything to do with me, he said. Not after I'd—he said I'd spread my legs for every outlaw this side of the border. That isn't true. I didn't. It was just . . . Bud. But Bud *made* me do it!"

"I know," Jessie said as soothingly as she could while gently brushing a disheveled strand of hair out of Polly's face. "You're going to be all right. We'll take you to a doctor."

"No," Polly murmured and her one open eye closed again. She shook her head. "I won't be all right. Clarence—he kicked me after he put me in here. I feel . . . I'm broken inside." Polly's left hand rose and touched her side, fell weakly back down to the ground. She grimaced. "I won't be all right ever again."

"Did you take the ruby brooch that Lomax had in his safe?" Jessie held her breath as she waited for Polly's answer.

A sigh escaped from between Polly's dry lips. It was followed by a thin trickle of blood.

"That brooch was mine originally," Jessie said.

Both of Polly's eyes opened this time, first the left, then the right. She almost smiled through the tears and the blood marring her face. "Pretty," she said softly.

"Did you take it?" Ki prompted, bending down to make sure that Polly would be able to hear him.

"*Yessss*." The word slipped away into meaningless sibilance.

"How did you manage to get into the safe?" Ki asked.

"I saw Bud open the safe—several times. I memorized the combination. It was a simple thing to do." Polly's eyes began to glaze. "Not like dying. Dying's a *hard* thing to do."

"What did you do with the brooch, Polly?" Jessie asked, giving Ki a glance that silently acknowledged the fact that Polly was slipping away from them.

" . . . needed money . . . for a new life for Clarence and me. The brooch . . . meant to sell it. But Clarence didn't want to go away with me."

Polly's eyes suddenly flared with a feverish fire. "He said he despised me for what I did—what I had become. He said he'd be better off without me. He had his career in politics to think of and a woman like me—a *whore* like me, he said— would ruin him. Oh, I think I could die easy if I thought he still loved me if only a little. It wasn't my fault what happened to me. Truly, it wasn't."

"I know that, Polly," Jessie said. "Do you think you can answer one more question for me? Please try to. What did you do with the brooch?"

"Nothing."

"Then you still have it?" Ki asked.

Polly shook her head—just barely. "Clarence . . . took it from me . . . said he intended to sell it. He said maybe something good would come out of the mess I'd made of our lives after all once he'd sold it. I thought if I gave him the brooch, he would be pleased. Pleased enough to forget about what had happened." Polly's eyes closed as her head slumped to one side.

"We've got to get her to a doctor, Ki. Stay here with her. I'll go find one and bring him here." Jessie sprang to her feet and was about to leave the cramped confines of the outhouse when Ki put out a hand and stopped her.

Then he reached down and placed two fingers on the white column of Polly's neck. "Jessie, she's dead."

Jessie and Ki left the outhouse—and saw Lomax leave the house and head toward them.

Keenly aware of Polly's pathetic corpse behind her, Jessie said, "It's time Lomax got what's coming to him." Her hand dropped to the butt of her gun.

102

"You're not going to shoot him, are you?" a startled Ki inquired.

"No. but that's what he deserves."

"What are you two doing out here?" the outlaw asked gruffly as he came striding up to Jessie and Ki.

"Talking to Polly Jessup," Jessie replied.

"You found her, did you?"

"We found her," Ki said flatly. He pointed to the outhouse.

Lomax stepped around Jessie and saw Polly. "What's wrong with her?"

"She's dead, that's what's wrong with her," Jessie informed Lomax. "When I talked to Jessup when we were here before, he said he had to go to the outhouse. Afterward, it occurred to me that the outhouse might be the place where we would find his wife. Now I realize he probably wanted to go there to hide her from us. That's why I thought she was here—not in the house."

"What'd she die of?" Lomax asked, stepping closer. When he saw the blood on Polly's face, he asked, "You killed her?"

"We didn't," Ki replied. "Jessup did."

"That's not quite correct, Ki," Jessie said. "Oh, it was Jessup who beat Polly to within an inch of her life when she came back, causing her subsequent death. But it was you, Lomax, who really killed her."

"What the hell are you talking about? I never laid a hand on her. You said yourself it was her husband did her in."

"But she wouldn't have died—not like this, not lying on the floor of a stinking outhouse—if you hadn't abducted her during your robbery of the town's bank. You set in motion the wheels that ultimately destroyed Polly Jessup. Not to mention the fact that you treated her like something less than human when she was with you."

"How the hell do you know how I treated her?"

"Never mind how I know." Jessie drew her gun.

Lomax looked down at it and then up again at her. "What are you fixing to do, woman?" A slow mirthless smile spread across his face. "I get it. The old double cross, eh? You just got your hands on the brooch Polly stole from me and now you're cutting me out of that particular game. That's it, isn't it?"

"That isn't it," Ki said sharply. "Polly didn't have the brooch when we found her. It was taken from her by her loving husband."

"We're going after Clarence Jessup," Jessie told Lomax, "to get the brooch back. But you're not going with us."

Lomax went for his gun.

Ki raised his right leg and sent his foot slamming into Lomax's face, simultaneously knocking the man to the ground and the gun from his hand. Before the outlaw could recover from the sudden and unexpected attack, Ki retrieved the dropped gun and leveled it at him.

"Tell him, Jessie," he said.

Jessie, knowing what Ki meant, told Lomax, "That brooch you stole from the gambler, James Barton. It's mine. Barton stole it from me. I mean to have it back."

Lomax got to his feet. He stood facing Jessie and Ki, one hand absently rubbing his jaw, on which a blue-black bruise, the result of Ki's martial arts' kick, was developing. "Look," he said. "You can have the brooch—if you can find Jessup and get it away from him. You're welcome to it. Only don't shoot me. What've you got to gain by shooting me, huh? I ask you now. Let me go. I won't ever cross your trail again. I promise you that. Just don't shoot me, okay?"

Jessie's finger tightened on the trigger. She wanted at that moment nothing in the world so much as to empty her gun into Lomax. To see the bullets tear into his bestial body and rip it apart. She wanted for Polly Jessup the revenge the dead woman could now never wreak on her tormentor.

"Jessie."

Ki had spoken her name softly and yet with an odd and compelling kind of force. He didn't touch her. He didn't even look at her.

But she understood and reacted. Her finger eased off the trigger. But she kept her gun aimed at Lomax's midsection. "March," she ordered. "We're going to the marshal's office."

"I can't tell you how glad I am to finally get him under lock and key," the marshal told Jessie and Ki as he returned from the cell block in the rear of his jail and hung his key ring on a nail that protruded from the wall. "That Lomax has been the bane of my existence for a good long time, not to mention a problem for the authorities in Arizona and New Mexico Territories. Matter of fact," he continued, sitting down in a chair behind his desk, "Lomax escaped once from Yuma prison. Well, he won't escape from my jail. I'm putting a twenty-four-hour-a-day guard on him. The deputy that lets him slip out of here is going to have to answer to me and when he's done doing his answering, he's going to find himself fired and looking for a new job."

"We thank you for sending your deputy to get the coroner to care for Mrs. Jessup," Jessie said.

"Only doing my duty, Miss Starbuck. But it's a sad one in the case of that poor woman. The only good thing to come out of all that you've told me is the fact that I finally got to meet the head of the Starbuck business empire that I've been hearing about for lo, these many years."

"The *really* good thing to come out of the Lomax affair," Ki said, "is that he won't be riding the owlhoot trail for a good long time. That ought to make folks rest easier in their beds in Texas and the territories you mentioned, marshal."

"There's something I'd like you to do for me, if you would be so kind, Marshal," Jessie said.

"Name it, Miss Starbuck, and I'll do it just as fast as ever I can."

"I'd like you to make it known to anyone who's willing to listen to you the fact that Clarence Jessup murdered his wife."

The marshal clucked and scratched his head. "That's another sad thing. About Clarence, I mean. I guess the man must have been a bit unhinged to do what he did to poor Polly."

Ki glanced at Jessie and saw the hectic flush that was reddening her cheeks. He readied himself for the explosion he was sure was coming.

"Clarence Jessup was not unhinged, Marshal," Jessie said in voice that could have frozen water in July. "He was a selfish and self-serving man who thought only of his own needs and desires. He wanted to run for governor of Texas, and the fact that his wife had been kidnapped and abused by outlaws did not fit in with his carefully laid plans, so when she returned he attacked her and stole from her a brooch of mine that she had hoped would, when transformed into cash, mean the start of a new life for her and her husband."

"I reckon you're right on the mark, Miss Starbuck, though it grieves me to say so. I always liked Clarence."

"But you'll make sure the newspapers in the area receive word of the murder Jessup committed?"

"I will, yes."

"I'm obliged to you." Jessie started for the door.

"What are you going to do about the fact that you told me—the fact that Clarence Jessup has your ruby brooch, Miss Starbuck?"

"I'm going after him and I'm going to get it back."

"You know, Miss Starbuck, somebody told me once—it was a man who had met you a while back—he said you were a rose made out of iron. At the time, I thought he was just spouting poetry at me. But now, after listening to you here today, I know exactly what the gentleman meant, and I have to say I think he was one hundred percent right."

On that note, Jessie and Ki left the marshal's office.

"Where are you going?" Ki asked Jessie once they were outside and she had freed her reins from the jail's hitch rail and begun to lead her horse down the street.

"Come on. We have a stop to make—at the livery barn."

When Ki, leading his own horse, caught up to her, he said, "You figure you can find out where Jessup went at the livery, I take it."

"It's a place to start. I saw no evidence at his home that he owned a horse. No barn. No tack shed. Not even a sack of grain. So if he has left town, he would have to rent or buy a horse or some kind of rig. My bet is he'd want to put enough distance between him and us, and a horse can do that for him better than any kind of rig can."

"You think he's skipped town?"

"I think he figured that we wouldn't be satisfied with what he told us about Polly—that he hadn't seen her. He probably knew we'd ask questions, and if we did, we'd find out sooner or later that Polly had returned to him. He knew we'd be back if we found out he lied to us, and even if we didn't find her in the outhouse where he'd left her, he also knew his life would be in danger from Lomax and his hair-trigger temper. In fact, he asked me if I was going to shoot him while you and Lomax were searching the house. To put a scare into him, I told him I wasn't going to shoot him but that Lomax probably would if he had lied to us about Polly's whereabouts."

When they arrived at the livery barn they found its cavernous front door flanked by idlers. All the men's eyes, some openly and some surreptitiously, appraised Jessie as she approached them.

"Good day, gentlemen," she greeted them.

"Dammit to hell" a whittler, who had white hair and a salt-and-pepper goatee, exclaimed as he shook his finger and drops of blood flew from a self-inflicted cut.

"You should mind your whittling," Ki said. "A slip of the knife and you could lose a finger."

Sucking on his cut finger, the whittler, unmindful of Ki's mild taunt, stared in wide-eyed admiration at Jessie.

"Would any of you men happen to know where I can find Clarence Jessup?" she asked the gathering.

"My guess is he'll be to home warming up his long-lost wife," one of the younger men answered with a gleam in his eye.

"That just goes to show how much you know," the whittler declared dismissively. "Jessup came in here an hour ago. That was before you got through painting your nose in the saloon across the street. He rented a buckskin and rode out of town."

"Maybe I should mosey over to his place and try warming up his wife for him so her pump'll be primed by the time he gets back," the younger man said, grinning now from ear to ear, the gleam in his eyes undimmed.

"That's no proper way to talk in front of a lady, whipper snapper," a codger perched on a cracker barrel declared with evident distaste. "You ought to be ashamed of yourself."

"Which way did Mr. Jessup head when he left the livery?" Jessie asked the whittler.

He pointed south with his bloody finger.

"Much obliged," Jessie said. Then she and Ki turned their mounts and rode away from the livery.

"I want to stop at the telegraph office," Jessie said before they had gone very far.

"Shouldn't we try to narrow the gap between Jessup and us as fast as we can?"

"We will. But I have some messages I want to send first."

When they drew rein in front of the telegraph office on their way out of town, Jessie dismounted, handed her reins to Ki and went inside.

When she came out some time later, there was an expression of self-satisfaction on her face.

"Do you mind my asking who you wired?"

"The governor. The head of the Republican party in

108

Texas. A few newspaper publishers in such places as Austin, Dallas and Fort Worth."

"My next question is why."

"I wanted to make sure they all knew that Clarence Jessup is now wanted for the murder of his wife. I wanted to make sure that he won't be able to hold his head up in respectable society for as long as he lives, never mind run for statewide political office."

★

Chapter 7

Jessie and Ki rode into Brownsville late that night without having found any trace of Jessup. Neither of them would admit to being discouraged or, worse, fearful that they would not find the man and the brooch they hoped he still had in his possession. They went directly to the livery and made arrangements to board their horses there for the night.

After giving the farrier instructions about the feeding and watering of the animals, Jessie gave the man a detailed description of Jessup and asked if he had seen him.

"Not me, personally, no, I didn't see him," the farrier replied, "but I heard about a fellow fits that description. He was here in town this afternoon. Folks told me he looked like he'd been doing some hard riding. He was asking everybody in sight if they wanted to buy some jewelry he had for sale."

Jessie felt her pulse quicken. "Would the jewelry the man had happen to have been a ruby brooch?"

"It was, as a matter of plain fact. You fixing to buy it, are you?"

"I'd like to see it," Jessie answered with careful ambiguity.

"Well, you've come a little too late for that, I'm afraid. That fellow, he left town."

"You mean he sold the brooch?" Ki inquired.

"No, he didn't get no takers for it. There's nobody in Brownsville has anywhere near the kind of money he wanted for the thing. When he found out he couldn't palm it off on anybody around here, he up and left town, like I said."

"How long ago was that?" Ki asked.

"No more than an hour or two ago, I'd say. The sun was just down when he went."

"Which way did he go?" Jessie asked.

"A fellow who was in here just before you two showed up said he went south. Seems he expressed the hope that he'd be able to sell the brooch somewheres down in Old Mexico."

"Thank you for the information," Jessie said wearily, feeling as if her pursuit of the Firebird was fast becoming an endless quest.

As they made their way out of the livery and down the street toward a hotel, she said, "Wait."

Ki halted as Jessie had just done. "What is it?"

"Maybe we shouldn't stop here tonight. Maybe we should hit the trail again."

"Jessie, I understand your eagerness to catch up with Jessup. But we've got to get some rest or we'll both be no good at trailing him. Besides it's pitch dark and I'm tuckered."

"I am too, I have to admit. It's just that I'm developing a feeling of desperation. My brooch—it seems to have taken on a life of its own. Just about the time we are close to getting our hands on it, it vanishes and we have to begin our hunt for it all over again."

"A good night's sleep will do us both good. We can

111

head out again at first light. Come on." Ki led the way to the hotel.

The following morning, after a hurried breakfast in the hotel's restaurant, Jessie and Ki crossed the street to the livery, where they found a young man in attendance who bore a decided resemblance to the farrier they had dealt with the night before.

"You're in charge here?" Ki asked.

"Yes, sir. My pa works days and I work nights. What can I do for you?"

"Our horses are here. In those stalls right over there. The blood bay and the black."

"I'll go get them, sir."

"Ki, look at this!" Jessie cried as she picked up a newspaper that sat atop a keg of nails. She held it up for him to see.

The front page, in enormous letters, announced that the Republican party of Texas had withdrawn from nomination for governor the name of Clarence Jessup.

"Looks like your telegraph messages got action," Ki said as he scanned the article that mentioned "the shock" the party felt upon learning "from informed sources" that their "promising gubernatorial candidate" was now "a hunted man wanted for the murder of his spouse."

The farrier's son returned, leading Jessie's and Ki's mounts, both of them saddled and bridled and looking rested and fit.

They paid him what they owed and led their horses out into the light of the rising sun. Having stepped into their saddles, they rode toward the edge of town.

Jessie drew rein when she heard a newsboy, as he hawked his morning newspapers, shouting out the news that Clarence Jessup had been, in the boy's far from elegant phrase, "dumped by the Republican party."

She fished a coin from her pocket and handed it to the

112

boy, who gave her a copy of the newspaper. She turned in her saddle and placed the paper in her saddlebag.

"A souvenir?" Ki asked.

"A present," she answered. "For Jessup when we catch up with him. In case he hasn't heard the bad news."

They rode out of town, heading south, both of them scanning the surrounding countryside and the ground around them for sign of Jessup. None was visible. When a flock of sparrows descended into some distant treetops and then immediately hurled themselves skyward again, Ki called Jessie's attention to them and then rode with her to the grove to investigate the birds' strange behavior.

"Something scared those sparrows," he pointed out to her as they neared the trees. "Better keep your hand on your gun, just in case."

They halted just outside the grove and listened but could hear nothing. They were about to ride in among the trees when Jessie said, "Someone's coming."

Ki reached for his rifle. Jessie's hand rested on the butt of her still-holstered .38.

A man emerged from the trees leading a packed mule. He stopped when he saw Jessie and Ki and pushed his sweat-stained felt hat back on his head. He was an elderly man with slightly bowed legs and eyes that perpetually squinted, suggesting their need for spectacles. His gray hair needed washing and his boots needed new heels.

"Howdy," he said cheerfully, his eyes darting to Jessie's and Ki's hands, which were on their guns. "No need to be hostile. Old Ames wouldn't hurt a fly, for fear it'd hurt him back." His laugh was a cracked cackle. "Where you headed, strangers?"

"South," Ki answered. "Did you happen to see anybody else heading in that direction?"

"Just one fellow all by his lonesome. Beanpole of a man. In a helluva—beg pardon, miss—hurry. It was when I came out of those hills yonder." Ames pointed to the east.

113

"Been prospecting up there for near to a week but haven't so much as got a speck of color to show for my efforts, sad to say."

Jessie described Jessup. "Was that the man you say you saw heading south?"

"Sounds a lot like him."

Jessie and Ki wheeled their mounts and resumed their journey. An hour later, after fording the Rio Bravo, they spotted a small Mexican village in the distance. It was composed of squat adobe buildings clustered around a plaza. The only structure to be seen that was taller than a single story was a church that towered above the village like a stork above a flock of chickens.

"We can ask after Jessup there," Ki said.

As they rode into the village, they saw a crowd of men, women and children in the plaza in front of the open bronze door of the church. A few of the women were weeping. Nearly all the men wore sullen expressions as they faced the priest who stood on the church steps as he spoke to them.

Jessie and Ki drew rein near a fountain some distance behind the assemblage but close enough to hear the words the priest was speaking to his parishioners.

"What's he saying?" Ki asked.

Jessie translated the priest's Spanish. "He says what happened is a cross the villagers will have to bear. He says it is unfortunate, but they must not despair at what happened. They must be strong. He says God will not give them a burden too heavy for them to bear."

"*Mentiroso!*" a man at the rear of the crowd called out, shaking a fist at the priest.

Shocked voices shouted him down in swift Spanish.

"What was that all about?" Ki asked Jessie.

"That man who shouted—he accused the priest of lying. The others denounced him—the man in the crowd, not the priest."

The man shouted again, and a woman near him, an

expression of utter shock on her face, crossed herself and cried, "*Madre de Dios!*"

"What did he say?" Ki asked.

"He told the priest that God has given the villagers not a heavy burden to bear but His curse. He said something about the colonel being a curse from God or, perhaps, from the Devil."

The priest bowed his head and then, squaring his shoulders as if to do battle with an unseen enemy, raised it again and blessed the crowd. Turning, his shoulders slumping, he disappeared into the church, where votive lights could be seen flickering like so many uneasy eyes in the dark.

Voices outside the church were raised in argument, most of them male. But the majority of the members of the crowd drifted away and disappeared around corners and into houses.

A young woman of striking beauty appeared. She had shining black hair that spilled down upon her shapely shoulders, which were revealed, as was her deep cleavage, by the off-the-shoulder white blouse she wore, equally black eyes that sparkled with an inner light, and finely sculpted bones that silently spoke of both Spanish and Aztec blood flowing in her veins. She smiled when she caught sight of Jessie and Ki sitting their saddles not far away from where she stood.

She approached them with the charming shyness of a doe discovered in a forest glade and said, *"Buenos dias."*

Jessie answered her in Spanish and then, in the same language, asked her, for Ki's benefit, if she spoke English.

"*Sí*, I do speak it, the English," the woman answered. "What is it brings you here to the village of Del Rio?"

"We are looking for a man," Jessie answered and described Clarence Jessup.

"Ah, then you have come to the right place, señorita. The man, he is here."

"Ki, did you hear?" Jessie cried, jubilation in her voice.

115

"I heard. Señorita—"

The woman smiled and shyly said, "My name, it is Marisol Ruiz."

"I'm pleased to meet you, Marisol," Ki told her and gave her his and Jessie's names. "Where is the man we have been looking for?"

"You will find him there." Marisol pointed to a low adobe building with one partially crumbled wall on which someone had crudely painted the word "Cantina." "But I do not think he will want to talk to you. He is very sad, the man. It is the fault of Don Demonio." Marisol's voice had dropped to a mere whisper as if she were afraid to speak the name she had just uttered out loud.

"Don Demonio?" Ki repeated, puzzled.

"Sir Devil," Jessie translated.

"Who is this Sir Devil, Marisol?" Ki asked.

"His name, it is Victoriano Amador. He calls himself 'Colonel,' but that is like me calling myself a princess. Untrue. He is a vain man and a bloodthirsty one. He makes our life here harder than it would be if he did not exist, and ours is a hard life to begin with."

"What do you mean," Jessie prodded, "When you say Colonel Amador is 'bloodthirsty'?" Her eyes were on the open door of the cantina in the distance.

"He and his men are bandits. They steal from us. They treat our women like animals. It makes the women ashamed and the men angry. One day there will be a rising. Our men will wake one day and they will say 'no more.' That is a day I dread."

"But surely you want to be free of this Colonel Amador?"

"Yes, that is so, señorita. But freedom can only be bought, where a man like Don Demonio is concerned, at a high price. A price that must be paid in young men's blood. A price that Death will collect. I have a brother, Diego. I love him very much. I do not want him to die. It is—how you say it in the English—it is a dilemmo."

"Dilemma," Ki corrected gently.

"*Sí*, a dilemma. We want to be free, but we are afraid to pay the price our freedom costs."

"We're sorry to hear of your trouble," Jessie said sympathetically. "But we must go now to the cantina."

"To see the man you seek?"

"Yes."

"He is another chicken like us for the colonel to pluck," Marisol declared sadly. "When comes the colonel once more to Del Rio earlier today, he and his men, they take our last two goats and cut their throats. Then they build a fire and roast and eat them. Now there are babies in Del Rio who will drink no milk this day or in the days to come. The colonel's men they turn to our women once their bellies are full." Marisol looked away, color rising in her cheeks.

"But what of—" Ki began.

"The gringo, *sí*. He is here when Colonel Amador comes like the locust to plague us. He sees the colonel's fine uniform, his polished boots. He sees the way many of the men and women of our village treat him like a feared king. He goes to the colonel. He shows him a jewel."

Jessie's breath caught in her throat.

"He says," Marisol continued, " 'this jewel I will sell to your honor.'

" 'No, you will not,' says the colonel to him. 'I will take it and thank you for your generous gift.' The colonel, he takes the jewel, and when the gringo cries out as if stabbed in the heart and tries to take it back, he gets, not the jewel, but Don Demonio's boot in his face."

Jessie softly sighed, feeling an overpowering sense of déjà vu as once more her hunt for her missing brooch ended and began again, all in the same moment. The Firebird that had been in the possession of Clarence Jessup was now in the possession of a Mexican bandit, and she was back where she had started, at the moment she first discovered that her

117

prized piece of jewelry was missing.

She turned and opened her saddlebag. After extracting from it the newspaper she had bought earlier, she excused herself and rode toward the cantina.

Ki, with a nod to Marisol, did the same.

They both dismounted and entered the cantina. Jessie called out, "Jessup!"

The man was leaning on the bar and pleading in a strident voice with the bored bartender. He did not turn at the sound of his name.

"Just one," he wheedled, holding up an index finger.

The man behind the bar ignored him as he ran a wet rag across the smooth surface of the plank propped up on two barrels that served as a bar.

"Please," Jessup pleaded with him. He reached across the bar and seized the bartender's shirt.

"*Un*," Jessup said. "*Uno. Unita?*" He swore. "What the *hell* is the Spanish word for one?"

The man behind the bar contemptuously slapped Jessup's hand away.

Jessie crossed the room and confronted Jessup.

"What do you want?" he cried in alarm, his gray eyes widening and filling with fear at the sight of her. He turned his head and saw Ki approaching him. He began to back away, holding out both hands as if to ward off an impending blow.

Neither Jessie nor Ki moved. They didn't speak.

Jessup collided with the wall. He stood there with his back pressed against it. He watched them watching him, his gaze shifting from one to the other. He looked as if he were about to weep.

"I haven't got it," he whimpered. "He took it. He took the brooch and he took my money and now that greaser behind the bar won't extend credit to me so I can't have a drink and I *need* one. Oh, great God in heaven, I need one *badly*!"

Standing there, a stricken look on his face, Jessup dropped his head into his hands. His shoulders began to shake.

Ki wanted to turn away from this spectacle of a man coming apart at the seams, but he didn't. Like Jessie, he continued staring at the distraught Jessup.

"I haven't got it," Jessup said, taking his hands away from his face. "A military man—he took it from me. So you've wasted your time tracking me down."

"We know that Colonel Amador took the brooch from you," Jessie said. She stifled the sense of pity she was feeling for Jessup by forcing herself to remember Polly as she lay dying on the floor of an outhouse in another town and another time. A cold rage replaced the pity. "We know what you did to your wife," she told Jessup. "You're now a wanted man."

"Nobody wants me," he moaned, wallowing in self-pity.

"You're wrong about that," Ki interjected. "The law wants you, and when the law gets you—and it will—you'll hang for the crime of murder."

Jessup looked away as if searching for some means of escape from an intolerable situation. Then, "I couldn't help myself. When Polly came to my office—when I first saw her—I was filled with loathing. She looked . . . debased. I rushed her out of my office. I asked her did they . . . bother . . . her. She *admitted* it. Wouldn't you think she would have had the common decency to lie to me about *that* to spare my feelings?

"When we got home, she showed me the brooch. She said she stole it from the leader of the outlaws who abducted her. She said we could sell it and use the money it would bring to make a new start in life somewhere else."

Jessup groaned and rolled his eyes like a steer that enters the slaughterhouse and knows fear but not yet why it feels that fear.

Jessie, watching him, could feel only disgust and no shame for feeling as she did.

"I hit her," Jessup confessed. "I don't know how many times I hit her. I wanted to punish her for what she had done to me. I wanted to make her *pay*! Did you know that I was going to run for governor of Texas? The party had enthusiastically endorsed me. There was a great deal of money made available by sundry sources to finance my campaign. I was on my way to fame and fortune, and then she—then Polly let herself be taken. She could have fought back. She could have run from those outlaws who were robbing the bank that day. Don't you think she could have run away from them?"

Neither Jessie nor Ki answered the question.

Jessup laughed, a horribly mirthless sound. "Can you imagine it? My lady Polly on my arm at the inaugural ball? Why, I would have been the laughing stock of the state!"

Jessup sniffed and wiped his nose with the back of his hand. "After it happened, after I'd hit her however many times I did in a fit of rage, I didn't know at first what to do. I wasn't thinking clearly. I picked her up, carried her upstairs—but I couldn't leave her there. I finally decided to hide her where you found her."

"In the outhouse," Ki said, his voice icy.

"Yes. Then you came. When I heard the sound of the front door being smashed to smithereens, I was on my way back from depositing Polly in the outhouse. I thought it must be the marshal come to claim me for what I had just done. My mind was on fire. I thought the marshal had found out what I'd done and it was all over for me. Then I saw the three of you."

"I couldn't believe what I was hearing—that you wanted Polly. That other man that was with you—where is he?" Not waiting for an answer, Jessup hurried on. "I had to lie. I couldn't tell you where Polly was. Nor could I tell you that I had the ruby brooch in my pocket at that very moment—the brooch Polly had given me. You would have taken it from me. And I . . . I needed it. It and the little

120

money I could scrape together on short notice to finance the flight I was planning."

Jessup moaned. "Now my money, the brooch—all gone. Stolen from me by that renegade who calls himself a colonel."

Jessie unfolded the newspaper in her hand and offered it to Jessup. Staring into her eyes, he took it from her and looked down at it. His lips moved as he read his fate printed there. He looked up again at Jessie.

"It's all over, isn't it?"

Jessie nodded.

Jessup seemed to dissolve, to shrink before her eyes. "I didn't want it to happen," he wailed. "None of it should have happened. The kidnapping in the bank—it wasn't my *fault*!"

He staggered forward, looking as if he were about to fall. But he managed to brush past Jessie and Ki and lean on the bar. "*Unito*?" He raised one finger and pointed at a bottle of brandy that sat on a shelf behind the bar. "*Unos*? Please! Won't you show a poor unfortunate man a little mercy?"

Jessie turned on her heels and walked out of the cantina so that she would not show the contempt she was feeling for Jessup. When Ki joined her outside, she said, "Let's talk to the priest. Find out what we can about this Colonel Victoriano Amador."

They had just started for the church when a young man approached them, with black hair and eyes, a mustache that drooped on both sides of his patrician lips, and skin the color of hickory.

Jessie, watching him as he strode toward them, was reminded of the *santos*, the carved figures of saints, she had seen in other Mexican villages like this one. There was about the ascetic-looking young man a melancholy air but also one of great strength that was not merely physical. His gaze was penetrating and he moved with authority. She found him compelling in a not unpleasant way.

"Señor, señorita," he said as he joined them. "I am Diego Ruiz. My sister, she tells me of you. She says you are man-hunters. This is so, *sí*?"

"I'm afraid your sister has made a mistake," Jessie told him. "We did come here looking for a man, but I don't think we could be called manhunters in the ordinary sense of that word. This is my friend Ki. My name is Jessie."

"A pleasure. But I am disappointed. I thought perhaps you had come here to hunt Don Demonio."

"It's odd that you should mention that, Diego," Jessie said. "We came here to find the American who is now in your cantina. But now that we have found him, we have learned that we must find Colonel Amador."

Diego frowned. "Forgive me, Jessie, but I do not under-stand what it is you say."

"It's really quite simple. The man in the cantina was in illegal possession of a ruby brooch that belonged to me. I came to get it back from him only to find—"

"Ah, now I understand. I see Don Demonio take the ruby brooch from the Americano just like he takes from us our few poor possessions. So now you must find the colonel and get it back. This is true?"

"It is true," Jessie agreed.

"It will be a difficult task. The colonel, he is a dangerous man."

"We gathered as much," Jessie said. "It is no wonder that you are all afraid of him."

Diego drew himself up, a haughty expression on his hand-some face. "*I* am not afraid of Don Demonio. Give me a sharp knife or a gun with the bullets inside, and I could kill him like I would kill *la cucaracha*." Diego raised one booted foot and slammed it down upon the ground to illus-trate his words.

"I think Colonel Amador would require a great deal more killing than a simple cockroach," Ki suggested.

"You think Diego Ruiz is not brave? Do you think he is

not man enough to do such a thing?"

"On the contrary," Ki said, "I think Diego Ruiz is more than man enough to do what he says he would like to do. That's self-evident to me."

Diego relaxed. His eyes, which had been afire, softened, but the fire in them did not go out as he glanced at Jessie. "You, a woman, will go in search of Don Demonio, Jessie?"

"Yes, I, a woman, definitely will."

"I see that you have the gun."

Jessie nodded.

Diego said, "Maybe the colonel's way is the right way. Maybe I am wrong to live like the rest of the people in Del Rio. Maybe I should ride a strong horse like the colonel and his men and go where I please as does the wind and do as I please as does the summer storm and live off the labor and lives of others like the poor fools here in Del Rio."

"You do not look like a cruel man," Jessie commented.

The fire was back in Diego's eyes as he said, "I can be cruel. If that is what it takes to step up out of the mud and stand closer to the stars—*sí*, I can be cruel. Sometimes I think I will leave here. Sometimes I think I will become rich and powerful. To do that, I tell to myself, I must go to the colonel and tell him I am his. If he will let me stay with him—ah, then the world will open its treasure house to me, and I, Diego Ruiz, will at last have a life worth living."

"What does your sister say about that?" Jessie inquired.

"Marisol says nothing, because I do not tell her about the dream I dream in the dark before sleep comes to me in my bed."

"Marisol loves you very much, Diego," Ki remarked. "She wouldn't want to see anything happen to you, and something very well might happen to you if you were to decide to throw in your lot with Colonel Amador and his bandits."

"You think so? What then do you think might happen to me if I stay here in Del Rio and the colonel comes and maybe one day kills me because he does not like the way I lick his boots? It could happen. Other men in Del Rio have died at the hands of Don Demonio."

Ki could think of nothing to say.

Jessie said, "It was a pleasure meeting you, Diego. If you'll excuse us now, we were on our way to talk to your priest."

"I will go with you and introduce you to Father Juan. Come with me."

Jessie and Ki accompanied Diego across the plaza and into the dim interior of the church, which was illuminated only by the light that filtered through two small stained-glass windows and a host of flickering votive candles in their red glass containers.

On the wall above the altar's tabernacle hung an image of the crucified Christ. The candles gave a warm glow to the old gold of which the six-foot-long figure was made. Their light glinted on the long spikes extending from the figure's crown of thorns, which encircled its bowed head.

"Padre," Diego said, his voice seeming overloud in the quiet church.

The figure of the priest, his tonsured head bowed in prayer in the front pew, stirred, turned and, seeing his visitors, rose and came toward them.

"Padre," Diego said when the priest had joined them, "these are two strangers who have come to our village. Jessie . . . and Ki."

"How do you do?" Father Juan said in a pleasant voice that was almost free of an accent. "I am Father Juan Anza. What can I do for you?"

"We came to learn what we could about Colonel Victoriano Amador, Father," Jessie said. She proceeded to explain the reason for her interest in the brigand.

"Then that lovely brooch was yours," Father Juan breathed when she had finished. "I caught a glimpse of it before he took it from the American stranger. A truly beautiful thing it was. You must be very sorry to have lost it."

"I am. Not so much because of the money the brooch is worth, although the amount is considerable, but because of the sentimental value it has for me. It has been in our family for many years."

"I fear you will never see it again."

"Oh, I fully expect to see it again," Jessie declared confidently. "That's why we came to you for information about Colonel Amador. We intend to hunt him down."

"My dear child," a shocked Father Juan exclaimed, alarm in his eyes. "You must not do such a dangerous thing. Your life might become forfeit as a result of such a rash endeavor."

"Jessie is a woman who fights," Diego volunteered. "See, Padre, a gun she carries on her hip."

The priest saw but did not seem to want to see. "Colonel Amador is a ruthless man, Jessie," he said solemnly. "Surely the brooch cannot mean so much to you that you would be willing to risk your life to regain possession of it."

"It means that much and more to me, Father."

"Then I cannot dissuade you from what I consider to be the foolish course you seem determined to pursue?"

"No, Father, you cannot."

"But you can tell us what you know about Amador," Ki said. "Anything and everything that might help us find him."

"Sit down," Father Juan said, and the four of them took seats in one of the pews. "Victoriano Amador is a child of poverty like so many in Mexico. He learned early to steal his food and any money he could get his hands on. His father—unknown. His mother—dead, may God rest her sad soul, of venereal disease at the tender age of seventeen. Victoriano lived on the streets from the age of four, if you can believe it. He learned the cunning of the cougar, the ferocity of the grizzly bear, the tenacity of the bird of prey.

125

All his life he has been a man of evil. But who am I to condemn him when I know what he has had to suffer to survive?"

"And prosper," Diego added with a sly smile.

Father Juan quoted: " 'For what is a man profited, if he shall gain the whole world, and lose his own soul?' "

"He will have enough food to fill his belly," Diego said bitterly, answering the priest's rhetorical question. "He will have a fine house to live in and first- not second-hand clothes, without holes in them and more than a single pair of shoes—"

Father Juan silenced Diego by holding up a trembling hand. "You are young and you have fire in your heart. That can be a good thing. It can also be a bad thing. Take heed, Diego, to the love of our Lord. He will not abandon you. Though His cross be yours, too, do not lose the hope of heaven by succumbing to the lure of sin."

Diego was about to speak, but the priest turned away from him toward Jessie and Ki. "They call Colonel Amador 'Don Demonio.' "

"We know," Ki said.

"Marisol Ruiz told us," Jessie explained.

"It is, I suppose, a fitting appellation," Father Juan said, shaking his head. "Sometimes I think of Victoriano as the Devil incarnate. He lives in a way that often lures our young men—and, unhappily, some of our young women as well— to his side. You heard Diego just now. The colonel, like Satan, lies in wait for the unwary."

"Where does he lie in wait, Father?" Ki inquired. "I mean, where is his headquarters, if he has one?"

"I think it is not a good thing to tell you that. I think to tell you that is to send you to your deaths."

"We appreciate your concern for our safety," Jessie said, "and we thank you for it. But, Father, it is imperative that I find Colonel Amador and recover my brooch. So please— tell us."

"I will show you where Don Demonio is," Diego cheerfully volunteered.

"No, Diego," said a stern Father Juan. When Diego was about to protest, he added, "I forbid you to go anywhere near the hacienda of Don Alonso de León. Diego, I suggest you stay here and pray to our Lord to give you the strength to resist temptation."

As Jessie and Ki followed Father Juan out of the church into the blinding light of the sun spilling down upon the plaza, the priest clucked his tongue and said, "Victoriano draws young men like Diego to him as sugar water draws ants. It is as if Victoriano is the sun and young men who want more from life than the good God has seen fit to give them are the flowers—you call them, what—ah, yes—sunflowers—that must turn their faces to that sun as it moves across the sky. I worry about Diego Ruiz. One day I fear I will awaken and he will be here no more. I will learn that he has gone to Victoriano for a gun and his share of dangerous, perhaps deadly, dreams."

"It is easy to see, Father," Jessie said, "if you will forgive me for saying so, why young men like Diego would want to escape a village like Del Rio. There is little here to hold them."

"That is not so, Jessie. There is family. There are blood ties. There is much to hold them here in Del Rio.

"Diego has a sister, as you know, who loves him and would mourn if he were to leave her for any reason, especially were he to go and become one of Victoriano's minions."

"Father," Ki said, "when you speak of the colonel, I notice you use his first name. I take it you know him well."

"Once upon a time I knew Victoriano well. We were friends together on the streets of Mexico City. Like Victoriano, I was also alone and without parents. Mine died in a cholera outbreak. I was ten years old when I first met

127

Victoriano. He was eleven. He taught me much. I blush now to think of all that he taught me. But he was, I say in truth, a good and steadfast friend to me. When I was hungry and had found no edible food in the garbage thrown out the back doors of restaurants where the *turistas* went, he would give me his—even the very little he often had. He protected me from the older boys who, when they could not pay a woman, prowled the streets looking instead for young boys like me. Yes, in those days Victoriano and I were friends. But then God called me and Satan called Victoriano. Now he comes to this village of Del Rio, I think, to torment me, to mock my God and His useless servant who, neither of us, can do anything to stop his depredations."

"You were going to tell us, Father, where to find your— I was going to say friend," Jessie said.

"Life is rich in irony, is it not?" Father Juan said in a self-mocking manner. "Can it really be that the servant of God and the servant of Satan are friends? Well, never mind.

"Go, if you must, to the hacienda of Don Alonso de León. Victoriano has driven the de León family away from their ancestral home, and now he and his men use it as their base of operations in this area. It is heavily guarded against attacks by the *rurales*, I am given to understand, but the *rurales* seldom go there. Victoriano pays them a monthly stipend to look the other way and leave him and his men alone."

"Where will we find the de León hacienda, Father?" Ki asked.

With a sigh, Father Juan gave them directions. Then he blessed them both. "*Vaya con Dios*, my friends. You will need God to go with you on this journey you feel you must make. Without Him—" He left his statement incomplete, turned and hurried back into his church.

Chapter 8

As Ki and Jessie were riding out of the village of Del Rio, they heard the sound of glass shattering. That sharp sound was quickly followed by a man's shrill scream.

"Those sounds came from the cantina," Jessie said as she wheeled her horse and started back the way they had come, with Ki beside her.

Ahead of them, his cassock swirling about his legs, Father Juan was running toward the cantina, from which the bartender had emerged to stand wringing his hands and then frantically point to the interior of the building.

When Jessie and Ki reached the cantina they dismounted and went inside to find Father Juan kneeling beside the prone body of Clarence Jessup, which lay on the dirt floor in front of the makeshift bar.

Blood was flowing freely from a jagged wound in Jessup's neck.

"He's cut himself from ear to ear," Ki said softly.

"Is he dead, Father?" Jessie asked.

At first the priest did not answer her as his lips moved in silent prayer. Then, getting to his feet, he nodded. "*Sí* he is dead."

The bartender took several tentative steps into his establishment and began to babble in Spanish, both his eyes and his words wild.

"What's he saying, Father?" Ki asked, avoiding the sight of the body on the dirt floor—the dirt floor that reminded him of another dirt floor where another body had lain—the outhouse floor which was the last resting place of the wife of the man who had just died in Del Rio's cantina.

"Pablo says he could do nothing to prevent what happened," Father Juan told Ki. "He says that the Americano seized a bottle of brandy when his back was turned. The Americano was mad, he says, for, when he turned, he was using the jagged neck of the bottle he had broken to slit his own throat. Before Pablo could take the weapon away from him, the Americano had done what he set out to do."

Jessie nodded, saying nothing, and then she and Ki started for the door.

"One moment."

They turned as Father Juan came up to them and said sternly, "Perhaps you should not try to regain possession of your brooch." He made a half turn and pointed to Jessup's corpse. "Look at the fate it has brought to him. Maybe it is accursed."

Jessie shook her head. "No, Father, it is not the brooch that did that." She indicated Jessup's corpse with a curt nod. "His own selfishness did that."

But she couldn't help wondering, as she and Ki boarded their horses outside the cantina and rode out of Del Rio, that of late the brooch had seemed to bring misfortune of one kind or another to each of the people who had possessed it, however briefly.

"There it is," Ki said some time later, pointing to the canyon that Father Juan had told them would lead them to the de León hacienda, which was now occupied by Colonel Amador and his men.

"I hope we make our way through it without being blown to bits in the process," Jessie said uneasily, looking up at the towering tops of the canyon's walls.

As they rode into the mouth of the canyon, they saw the brilliant flash of light that had come from the mesa on their left. It was immediately followed by another one a mile farther on.

"Heliograph," Jessie said. "Somebody up there is sending signals to the hacienda that they've got visitors."

"Well, that's better than getting shot at," Ki remarked with a bemused grin.

They rode on and soon heard the sound of horses' hooves in the distance ahead of them. Moments later, as five horses and the Mexicans riding them came into sight around a bend in the canyon, they drew rein and waited for whatever was about to happen next.

The leader of the advancing men brought his horse to a halt and held up a hand, a signal to the men with him to do the same, which they promptly did. He was a tall, lean man with long black hair and deeply set eyes which, although they were also black, seemed to blaze. His cheeks were sunken and his mouth was a thin grim line like a knife wound in his face. His forehead, what could be seen of it beneath his wide-brimmed sombrero, was heavily lined, and his nose showed signs of having been broken in the past. He spoke to Jessie and Ki in Spanish.

Jessie answered him in the same language and then, switching to English, added, "It would be a favor to my friend—and much appreciated—if you would speak English if you can. He doesn't understand Spanish."

The leader of Amador's riders glanced at Ki with an unmistakable expression of contempt, whether because Ki could not speak Spanish or for some other reason, it was impossible to say. "What blood beats in your friend's veins?" the man asked, returning his attention to Jessie.

"His name is Ki and he is half-American and half-Japanese, if that's any of your business," she answered.

The man's eyebrows rose. He nodded his head, his lips

131

pursed. "Those who come into this canyon—they are my business. Who are you? What do you want here?"

"My name is Jessie. Ki and I have come here to see Colonel Amador."

"For what reason do you come?"

"I'll tell that to the colonel," Jessie said sharply, "not to one of his hired hands."

"You call Paco Valdez a 'hired hand'? Your insolence is exceeded only by your beauty, Jessie."

"Call it insolence if you like. I call it a matter of good sense. Why deal with hired hands when it is the boss you want to talk to?"

Valdez shook a stiff finger at Jessie. "Be warned, woman. You do not talk to a man like that—not this man, you do not. I could kill you both in the blink of an eye and leave your bodies here for the vultures to feed on. Is that what you want?"

"Jessie has already told you what we want," Ki replied, "which is to talk to Colonel Amador. We have something to say to him that we think he will want to hear."

Valdez snorted. He pulled his sombrero down low on his forehead, sending shadows scurrying down to his chin and making his features difficult to see. But it was not difficult to hear the annoyance in his tone when he curtly snarled, "Follow me," wheeled his horse, and rode back the way he and the men with him had come.

They parted to let him pass and then fell in behind Jessie and Ki, who were riding close behind him.

Minutes later, they emerged from the canyon into a large verdant valley. At its far end stood the de León hacienda with its back nearly pressing up against the hill that rose behind it.

"Señor de León must have been a smart man," Ki said to Jessie as they continued following Valdez. "He built his home all the way over there so that anyone out to cause him trouble would have this long stretch of table land to

132

cross before they could get near him. Which would give him time to mount an effective frontal attack on any such invaders."

"It's easy to see why this setup suited Colonel Amador," Jessie said. "Nobody's going to ride in here and take him by surprise. Even if they got past the pickets up on the mesa with their heliograph, they'd be mowed down no doubt before they could get close to the hacienda."

When Valdez brought his horse to a halt in front of the building and dismounted, Jessie and Ki did the same. Valdez's men melted away, some to a corral on the right side of the hacienda, others to a cluster of small adobe structures that were little more than mud huts. Valdez gave no signal and he spoke no word as he entered the hacienda, so Ki and Jessie followed him inside, across a courtyard filled with flowers and into a room at the end of a passageway.

Valdez spoke in Spanish to the huge, gaudily uniformed man who was seated behind a table on which were many dishes piled high with food—tortillas, rice, beans, roast beef and brown bread. The man leaned on the table with both elbows. His eyes, which were almost obliterated by the thick folds of flesh above and below them, peered at Jessie and Ki, to whom Valdez gestured as he spoke.

The man at the table was Victoriano Amador, Jessie knew, because of his uniform and because Valdez had addressed him as Colonel. He thrust a forkful of meat into his mouth and chewed it slowly as he continued to stare at her, almost totally ignoring Ki. His thick lips shone with a thin film of grease, as did one of his two chins. His pudgy hands held a knife and fork as a child might hold its most precious toys—lovingly, carefully. His plump cheeks quivered as he chewed. Sweat beaded on his forehead, to which some of his thinning black hair was plastered.

"What do you have to say to me?" he asked in heavily accented English after swallowing and then belching.

"We have heard about you, Colonel Amador," Jessie

133

answered. "My friend Ki and I—my name is Jessie, Colonel—have heard glowing reports of your valiant deeds and great courage."

Amador's eyes flickered. "So?"

"So," Jessie continued suavely, "we have come to join forces with you." A pause and then, "If your terms are satisfactory."

Amador grunted. "Why do I need you two? You can tell me this?"

"You need people who are good with guns," Ki said. "We are."

"I do not need a woman who is good with a gun," Amador said and shoved an overloaded spoonful of rice into his mouth. When he had chewed and swallowed, he added, "I need a woman only to scratch me when I itch down here." He made a point of making sure Jessie saw him grab his crotch.

"You need this woman," Ki said, indicating Jessie. "She can shoot the eagle off an American gold coin and leave it in still-spendable condition."

"Why do you not practice your shooting in *el norte*?" Amador asked. "Why do you come south to shoot?"

"Things are too hot for us north of the border right now," Ki answered. "We used to ride with the Lomax gang in Texas, but Lomax is in jail and his people scattered, so we came south looking to hook up with somebody like yourself where we'd be out of reach of the Texas Rangers."

Jessie said, "When we heard about how you and your men plundered the village of Del Rio, we decided you were the man we wanted to ride with."

"For a fair share of the profits from such plundering," Ki added.

"We heard about the ruby brooch you took from the American who was present during your visit to Del Rio. Now that, Colonel, was a real coup, a real piece of good luck."

Amador beamed at Jessie. "Worth a fortune is that brooch. As you say, a stroke of good fortune put it in my possession."

"Del Rio," Ki said, "wasn't so fortunate, I gather. The villagers said you took everything of value they had."

"That is not true," Amador said, gnawing on a bone. "There are still some things of value remaining in Del Rio which I have not yet seen fit to take."

Valdez grinned and spoke a name: "Marisol Ruiz."

Amador dropped the denuded bone onto his plate, kissed the tips of his fingers and then gestured with them. Then he spoke to Jessie. "You will show me how good you can shoot, yes?"

It wasn't, she realized, a request but an order. "Yes, Colonel, I will show you."

Amador heaved himself to his feet. Moving swiftly and surprisingly gracefully for a man of his bulk, he rounded the table and went out into the courtyard. There he called for Valdez, who hurried to him and gave an order.

Valdez bent down and picked up several small pieces of a crumbling flagstone. "Are you ready?" he asked Jessie.

When she nodded, he tossed a stone into the air.

She fired a round, which caused it to explode in midair.

Amador said nothing, but there was admiration in his eyes—as well as surprise. He gestured to Valdez, who promptly threw another stone into the air.

Jessie pulverized it with her second shot.

Amador, awed by her skill, muttered something under his breath. "What about your skill at shooting from a moving horse?" he asked. "To hit targets standing still on firm ground, that is one thing. But if you were fleeing for your life—what then?"

Jessie thumbed two bullets out of her cartridge belt and used them to fill the empty chambers in her .38. "I will tell you when to throw a stone, Valdez," she said and left the courtyard.

When the three men had joined her outside the hacienda, she was in her saddle, the reins in her hands.

"Begin," Amador barked.

Jessie slammed her heels into her bay's flanks and it went galloping away. When she had gone a good fifty yards, she turned the bay and galloped back the way she had come. When she was still some distance away from the men, she shouted, "Now, Valdez!"

He threw another stone into the air.

Jessie rode under it, turned in her saddle, took aim and fired. She shot the stone out of the sky.

When she had rejoined the men, Ki was smiling. Amador was staring at her as if she were a kind of creature he had never seen before. Valdez muttered something about "luck."

"That shooting, Valdez," said Amador, "was not luck. Not three times in a row, it was not. Jessie is—what is it they call such a one in the English?"

"A sharpshooter," Ki told him.

"Just so," Amador agreed and, to Jessie's surprise, he threw both arms around her and hugged her until she could barely breathe. Then, releasing her, he held her out at arm's length and kissed her wetly on both cheeks.

"You will ride with Colonel Amador's army," he declared expansively. "We will be proud to have you among us."

"Hold on," Jessie said as Amador let her go.

"Something?" he asked, his brow furrowing.

"Something," she repeated. "How much will you pay?"

"You will be paid as are my other soldiers."

"How is that?" she persisted, not really caring but knowing she had to put on a display of avarice for Amador's—not to mention Valdez's—benefit.

"My men and me, we have an arrangement. Fifty percent of our income goes to the men, to be divided equally among them. Ten percent goes to my good friend, Valdez. Forty percent is mine."

136

"How many men ride for you?"

"Nine."

"Now you have eleven of us," Ki declared.

Amador gave him a stormy look. "I do not recall having hired you."

"But—" Ki began, taken aback.

"I have just hired *her*," Amador said, pointing to Jessie. "I have done so because she has proved herself to me this day. I have seen with my own two eyes what she can do. How she can shoot. How she can ride and shoot at the same time. What can you do that will be of value to me?"

"I can shoot reasonably well," Ki offered. "I can fight."

"Ah, so you can fight, can you?" Amador stroked his chin as he gazed intently at Ki. "With your fists, you fight, yes? As do the gringo dogs in their saloons and back alleys?"

"If necessary I fight with my fists," Ki admitted. "But usually I fight using martial arts techniques I learned in Japan."

"I see. You are from Japan and you know how to fight as the Japanese do. Valdez here, he does not know how to fight in such a foreign manner. You, Ki, have you ever fought the way Mexican men sometimes fight?"

"I don't know what you mean."

"Then I shall tell you what I mean. The kind of fighting I have in mind, it is a test of a man's heart and his muscles. It is also a test of his will and his nerve. It is a fight with knives of which I speak. Knives and so simple a thing as a scarf."

"Oh, no," Jessie cried, realizing what Amador was referring to. "Ki, don't."

He chose to ignore her. "You're talking about the way Mexican men have of fighting each other with knives in their hands and their free hands gripping the ends of a scarf which keeps them close to one another."

"Just so," a beaming Amador said, rubbing his fat hands together. "You can fight in such a manner? Before you

137

answer, let me warn you. Valdez is a skilled knife-and-scarf fighter. He has killed more men in such fights than I like to think about."

Valdez's face remained impassive.

"Bring the knives," Ki said.

"Ki, don't," Jessie pleaded, going to him and putting a hand on his arm.

"Bring the scarf," he said, removing Jessie's hand from his arm.

"You are sure you want to do this thing?" Valdez asked him, his voice taunting his potential opponent as Amador returned to the hacienda to get the knives.

"I want it."

"Then I, too, must warn you, man of Japan. We have a saying here in Mexico. *Quien llama el toro aguanta la cornada.*"

"Which means?"

"He who calls the bull must endure the horn wound," Jessie said, translating Valdez's words. "Ki—"

But whatever she had been about to say was cut off by the returning Colonel Amador, who boomed, "I bring you brave gentlemen two deadly teeth with which you may try to bite each other if you can." He held the gleaming knives high above his head to reflect the sunlight.

Then, lowering the blades, each of which had been hand-wrought and ground to a razor-sharp double edge, he spoke to Ki. "You know, do you, that the first man to let got of the scarf is the loser?"

"I know."

"Then you may also know that the winner has the right by the rules of this little game to kill the loser."

"I know," Ki repeated and accepted the buckhorn-handled knife Amador gave him.

Valdez loosened the dirty sash he wore around his waist in place of a belt and flicked it toward Ki, who caught the free end of it and gripped it tightly. He waited as Amador gave Valdez the remaining knife.

Valdez, gripping the knife in his right hand, stepped backward, causing the sash to grow taut between himself and Ki. Then, with no warning, he lunged at Ki, his blade flashing in the sun.

Ki deftly twisted his body so that the thrust went wide. Then he parried Valdez's second attempt to stab him by bringing his own knife down in a sharp arc. Valdez made no sound as his shirt sleeve and then the flesh of his left forearm were slashed by Ki's knife.

Both men began to circle each other, the sash stretched tight between them. Ki danced nimbly out of the way of Valdez's sudden lunge, and again he ripped the flesh of his opponent's left forearm. This time Valdez let out an involuntary yelp and then clamped his mouth shut, his face darkening either from rage or embarrassment or a combination of both. Warily, the two men faced each other, prancing at times like boxers, standing stolidly in place at other times, the double-edged blades in their hands gleaming, Ki's stained with Valdez's blood.

Valdez was breathing heavily, his lips drawn back over his teeth as his eyes darted from Ki's knife to his face and then back to his knife again. Ki was ready for him when Valdez suddenly rushed him. He adroitly stepped to one side while maintaining a firm grip on the sash. But Valdez, not to be denied blood this time, determinedly swiveled in the direction Ki had moved and swung his blade, the tip of which punctured Ki's left bicep.

Intense pain erupted where Valdez's knife had penetrated Ki's flesh, but he ignored it, swiftly retaliating with an upward thrust of his knife while simultaneously jerking on the sash to draw his opponent closer to him and his blade. Valdez managed to sidestep, and Ki's knife cut only air. Before he could try again, Valdez put out one booted foot and tripped him. Ki went down hard but he did not release his hold on the sash, which was now flecked with blood. As Valdez raised his knife to deliver another blow, Ki jerked hard on the sash and Valdez fell on top of him.

Ki pushed Valdez aside, scrambled to his knees and was about to stab Valdez when the man managed to wrap the sash once around Ki's knife hand. Momentarily prevented from attacking his assailant, Ki fought to free his hand of the sash. As he did so, Valdez leaped to his feet and his knife sped downward toward Ki's body. To defend himself, Ki bent down low and, his shoulder hunched, used it to deflect the descending blow. As his shoulder struck the underside of Valdez's wrist, Valdez screamed a string of obscenities and, his balance lost, fell to the ground.

Ki sprang to his feet. His hand and knife came free of the sash. "You couldn't stick a trussed-up pig with that knife of yours, Valdez," he taunted, knowing that a madman was often a reckless man and that a reckless man took chances and often made dangerous mistakes. Valdez, still on the ground, slashed at Ki's legs but succeeded only in cutting a piece of leather from the heel of Ki's right boot. He tried a second time to trip Ki, but Ki was too fast for him. Then, as Ki hauled him to his feet by means of the sash, Valdez made a feeble effort to cut him again but failed to do so. Ki's blade swooped upward and entered the flesh of Valdez's left shoulder. Valdez screamed and frantically struck out, obviously aiming this time for Ki's eyes. Ki's head swiveled out of the way of the man's blade but not before it had ripped open the lobe of his right ear.

Valdez tried again for Ki's eyes, and Ki, enraged at the man's attempts to blind him so that he could kill him more easily, moved in on Valdez. His knife was about to descend and dip deep into Valdez's vulnerable gut when Amador shouted, "Enough!"

Ki's hand froze.

Valdez dropped his end of the sash and stepped backward, wiping the sweat from his face with his free hand.

Amador strode up to the two warriors. "I want neither one of you dead. We shall call this fight a draw. Both of you are valiant men. It would be a shame to lose either one of you."

"Then I've passed your test?" Ki asked, sucking air into his lungs. "You'll take me on?"

Amador threw his arm around Ki's shoulder. "With great pleasure, my friend."

Jessie, standing some distance away, breathed an audible sigh of relief that the knife fight was over and that Ki had not been hurt worse than he was. "Colonel," she said, forcing her voice to stay steady, "my friend needs bandages and an antiseptic if you have them."

"Yes, of course, Jessie," Amador declared expansively "You and your friend can share that adobe there." He pointed to one some distance from the main house. "I will send to you what you need."

Jessie went to Ki, and together they made their way to the building to which Amador had assigned them. They found it to be none too clean and only sparsely furnished. Jessie sat Ki down in a handmade chair next to a rickety table and then picked up a pitcher, from which a spider scurried, and took it to the well on the far side of the hacienda, where she filled it.

When she returned to the adobe, she found there a young woman who had brought a bottle of antiseptic and some clean cloths. When the woman had departed, Jessie proceeded to wash Ki's wounds and then douse them with antiseptic. Half an hour later, Ki was bandaged and in his own words, "feeling fitter than I did before the fight."

"I don't believe that for one minute."

"Well, maybe I feel about half as fit as before."

"That sounds more likely. I think you've made yourself an enemy."

"You mean Valdez."

Jessie nodded.

141

"If looks could kill, I'd be dead by now. Did you see the way he looked at me after Amador stopped the fight? His look had a sharper edge to it than did the knife he stabbed me with during the fight."

"You'd do well to steer clear of him."

"To change the subject—how do you want to go about trying to recover the Firebird?"

"I think we should try searching the hacienda. It might be there someplace. You heard Amador admit during his dinner that he did indeed have it."

"Maybe he posts guards at night."

"We'll have to see, won't we? If he does, well, we'll have to find a way of getting into the hacienda without being seen nor heard."

Late that night, following a communal supper presided over by Colonel Amador in the hacienda's dining hall, Jessie and Ki left their quarters and went out into the moonlit night. They stood just outside their door and listened to the sounds of snoring coming from the adobe nearest to the one they shared, the hunting howl of a coyote, which was answered by another coyote, and the creak of ropes that supported a hammock slung between two trees, in which one of Amador's men slept, his hands folded across his ample girth.

Moving swiftly and silently, the pair crossed to the entrance to the hacienda—and almost came face-to-face with one of the colonel's men, who was armed and seated on a wooden chair just inside the entranceway, his sombrero covering his eyes as he dozed.

They backed away from the man, flattening their backs against the walls on either side of the entrance. Ki motioned to Jessie, indicating a clay urn that sat on a ledge to his left and then to indicate that she was to take cover around the corner of the building.

When she had done so, he made his way to the urn and

toppled it, and, when it shattered on the ground, he raced around the side of the hacienda, then around to the back of the building, and rejoined Jessie where she had taken refuge.

"Let's go!" he said, taking her by the hand and leading her back to the entrance to the hacienda while the man who had been guarding it stood over the fallen urn and peered at it as if it could give him an explanation for its sudden demise.

Ki led Jessie into the courtyard and then into the dining hall that opened off it. "That guard won't come looking for us in here," he whispered. "He'll keep his eye out for anyone on the outside of the building as a result of what I did to decoy him away long enough for us to get inside."

"I'll take this room," Jessie said, "and then search the kitchen. You check the other rooms on the ground floor and meet me back here as soon as you can."

Ki moved like a silent shadow through the dining hall and out the door at its far end. When he had gone, Jessie began opening drawers in the sideboard that stood against one wall. She found that they contained only silverware bearing the de León family crest and stacks of white napkins that seemed to glow in the moonlight streaming through the windows.

She opened shallow drawers in the huge mahogany dining table but found that the Firebird was not in any of them. She began moving ornately framed pictures that hung on the walls, and which depicted, she supposed, the de León ancestors, to see if a wall safe might be hidden behind any of them. None was. She made her way into the kitchen and hurriedly checked through bins and clay pots and tin cannisters in search of her brooch but in vain. When she returned to the dining hall, Ki was waiting for her.

"Did you find it?" she asked him.

He shook his head and pointed to the ceiling. They made their way out of the dining hall and down the hall to the steps that led to the second floor. One of the steps creaked under their weight as they ascended, and they went rigid, afraid to move, afraid that if they did the sound, which had seemed like thunder to them in the otherwise quiet house, would bring Colonel Amador bounding out of his bed to catch them in the act of searching his quarters.

When no one appeared, they resumed their ascent and then, after a whispered conference on the landing, separated to search the bedrooms on that floor, Jessie going to the right, Ki to the left.

She searched an empty bedroom, examining the contents of a bureau, feeling the bed's mattress for any suspicious bulge and even upending the water pitcher, which contained neither water nor her brooch.

Outside in the hall again, she made her way to the next door and cautiously turned its knob. She was about to enter the moonlit room when she heard someone snore and realized she had been about to blunder into the room occupied by Amador himself, who lay, his naked bulk a small mountain, on a bed near the window.

She quickly withdrew and shut the door behind her. She stood there in the hall, waiting for her heart to stop pounding. She was still standing there a few minutes later when Ki rejoined her and gave her the disappointing news that her brooch was nowhere to be found.

She drew him away from the door of Amador's room and told him that she believed the brooch had to be in the colonel's bedroom. "We've looked everywhere else," she said. "It's got to be there. But so is he."

"Maybe we could search the room during the day, when Amador's not there," Ki suggested.

Jessie shook her head. "That would do only half the job. It wouldn't give us a chance to examine the clothes Amador was wearing when we searched his room. If we search the room now—the room *and* his clothes—I feel sure we're bound to find it. Besides, I want to finish what we've started. I want to get my brooch and get out of here. I

144

hate this place. This place and the people in it. I'll go in and search the room and the colonel's clothes while you stand guard."

"Be careful," Ki said softly, but Jessie was already inside the room.

She stood stock still, only her eyes moving, as they noted every item in the room.

A bureau. Two chairs. The bed and its fleshy burden. Clothes and boots in a pile on the floor.

She also noted what was not in the room. No overstuffed furniture. No water pitcher or basin. No pictures on the walls. No storage trunk.

She eased over to the bureau and opened the top drawer and found dirty underwear in it. A bandanna. A box of .38-caliber shells. The other drawers contained shirts, trousers, gold braided epaulets, socks. She went to the closet door near the bed and slowly turned its knob with both hands. Then, easing the door open, she began to search through the few clothes she found inside the closet. She found Mexican coins in the pocket of a pair of trousers. She found a metal toothpick in a shirt pocket. She didn't find the Firebird. She left the closet and knelt on the floor where Amador had dropped the clothes he had been wearing before he retired for the night. She went through them methodically, pocket after pocket, her hopes sinking when she found them all empty.

Then her hand hit on something hard in the colonel's vest pocket. Her fingers blindly felt its familiar facets. She touched the gold pin on the back of the object she had found. She knew, even before she withdrew it and held it up in the moonlight coming through the window, that she had at last and finally found what she had been searching for for so long—her ruby brooch.

She rose, turned—and stumbled over Amador's boots. The brooch flew from her hand as she fell. It went skittering across the pegged floor.

"Que hay?" Amador mumbled, sitting up in bed. "Ah, it is you, my pretty Jessie!" he exclaimed and reached for her. "What a pleasant surprise it is to see you here in my room in the middle of this long lonely night."

He pulled Jessie up to sit beside him on the bed. "You come to me like a pleasant dream. What happened? Did you stumble over something?"

"Yes . . . I did. Your boots . . . "

"Did you hurt yourself when you fell down?" Amador's cold fingers touched Jessie's cheeks, her lips, her nose.

"I'm all right."

"Lie down here with me. Do not be afraid, my pretty one. I will not hurt you. I will gladly give you what you came to me to get." Amador's shaft towered above his belly as he kissed Jessie on the lips. "Do not pull away from me like that, pretty one."

Jessie rose from the bed.

"You like to tease a man, yes?" Amador also rose and reached for Jessie. As he did so, he saw the brooch lying on the floor in a patch of moonlight. His eyes widened. He began to growl. He sized Jessie by the arm. His growl grew louder. "Dominguez!" he bellowed as he disarmed Jessie.

Ki burst into the room. "Ah, there you are, Jessie. I've been looking for you ever since we got separated downstairs. I see you've found Colonel Amador. Have you told him what we came to talk to him about?"

Jessie, quickly picking up Ki's cue, said, "No, I haven't had a chance to—"

"Dominguez!" Amador roared once more, brandishing Jessie's gun.

"Colonel," Ki began, but he was interrupted by the arrival of the man who had been guarding the entrance to the hacienda.

"Dominguez, you useless fool!" Amador roared. "You let these two thieves into my house to steal me blind. If I had not caught this one" —he shook Jessie so hard that her teeth

146

chattered— "she might have murdered me in my bed!"

Ki's hand slipped into his pocket, emerging with a throwing star.

"Seize him!" Amador bellowed.

Dominguez did, holding Ki in a bear hug that robbed him of breath and forced him to drop the *shuriken* in his hand.

"Take them to the cellar!" Amador ordered, releasing Jessie and picking up the dropped brooch. He held it close to her face and said tauntingly, "This was the prize the pretty one almost gained." The forced smile that had been on his face for a moment vanished. "For this you will die in the morning. You and your friend—I will personally shoot you both down like dogs. Dominguez, lock them in the cellar and bring me the key."

Domenguez let go of Ki and drew his revolver. Motioning with it, he marched Jessie and Ki out of the room as Amador, behind them, returned Jessie's Firebird to his vest pocket, from which she had taken it.

★

Chapter 9

"Damn!" Jessie muttered as the heavy wooden cellar door slammed shut behind her and Ki, leaving them in total darkness. "If only I'd been more careful and hadn't fallen over Amador's boots!" she lamented as Dominguez, outside their makeshift prison, turned a key in the lock.

Ki felt his way through the darkness to the door and placed his shoulder against it. He shoved; it didn't budge.

"I had the Firebird in my hand," Jessie said, her voice sounding sepulchral in the damp darkness of the cellar. "And now it's gone again."

"If you'll forgive me for saying so, your brooch is the least of the problems on our list at the moment. We're scheduled to attend a shooting. Ours."

"We've got to get out of here," Jessie said. "The question is how. Maybe we can break down the door."

"Forget that idea. It's solid as a rock."

"And there are no windows in here."

Ki felt his way along the wall next to the door. "The walls are dirt. If we had time, we could tunnel our way up and out of here. But we've not got time for that."

"Then what are we going to do?" Jessie moved through the darkness toward the spot from which Ki's voice had

148

come. She struck her shin on something, and the pain of the encounter brought tears to her eyes. "Ki, where are you?"

"Here."

She limped toward him, and they stood there in the utter darkness, their closeness a small comfort in the face of the apparent hopelessness of their situation.

They were seated with their backs against the earthen wall hours later when they heard footsteps outside the door of their prison. They both got to their feet and waited, listening to the rasp of a key in the door's lock. They clamped their eyes shut as the door swung open and the light of a lamp in Colonel Amador's hand blinded them.

Valdez, who was standing next to Amador with a revolver in his hand, smirked as Ki held up an arm to block the lamp's light. "I want to be the one to shoot him," he said, pointing at Ki. "You can have the woman, Colonel."

"I would like to have the woman," Amador said with a smile, his free hand coming to rest on the butt of Jessie's gun, which he wore in his waistband. "I would like very much to have her. Last night, when I awoke and found her in my room I thought she had come to me for love. But such, sad to say, was not the case. The thieving bitch had come to steal the jewel I took from the gringo in Del Rio. Take her and her friend outside."

Valdez stepped into the cellar and rammed the barrel of his gun into Ki's ribs. "Move, man of Japan. You too, woman."

Amador, holding the lamp high as if concerned that his prisoners might slip on the steps and hurt themselves, preceded them up the steps with Valdez right behind.

When they reached the main floor, Amador blew out his lamp and left it behind as Valdez marched Jessie and Ki outside into the almost white light of a searing sun that had just cleared the horizon. "Dominguez!" he called out, and the man who had been guarding the hacienda the night before detached himself from a group of Amador's men who had gathered to watch the execution of Jessie and Ki.

"You want me to kill them, Colonel?" a grinning Dominguez asked eagerly when he was face-to-face with his leader.

"No, I do not," Amador answered. "*I* want to kill *you*."

Dominguez's face fell. He tried a laugh that died in his throat. There was fear alive in his eyes. "A joke, Colonel? You make the joke, yes?"

"I make the joke, no. You let these two thieves get into the very heart of my home last night. For that you will pay with your life."

Dominguez went for the gun on his hip.

Valdez fired a single shot that blew off the smallest finger on the man's gunhand.

Dominguez screamed, startling a flock of mourning doves and sending them flying up from the red-tiled roof of the hacienda. He continued screaming as he dropped his gun and gripped his mutilated hand. He stared down at the bloody remnant of his finger that lay on the ground some distance away.

Amador gave an order, which did not seem to register with the now-whimpering Dominguez.

"Move!" Valdez barked.

Dominguez, moving like a man sleepwalking, went to the wall of the hacienda and pressed his forehead against it.

"Turn around!" Amador ordered, and Dominguez did, to reveal tears streaming down his face.

"Another chance," he whined, his eyes on Amador. "You must give me another chance, Colonel."

"I must give you nothing. Nothing but death. Now, stand up straight like a man."

Dominguez's eyes squeezed shut. His shoulders slumped.

"You two," Amador said, addressing Jessie and Ki. "Join my former friend Dominguez at the wall, if you please."

As Jessie walked with Ki to the wall, she couldn't help

thinking that Amador's last sentence had been spoken with an excess of politeness, which mocked her and Ki's desperate situation. When she reached the wall, she stood with her back against it, her head held high, Ki on her right, Dominguez some distance away from her on the left.

She blinked as a flash of light suddenly brightened the morning. She looked up as another one came from the mesa in the distance. The heliograph, she thought.

"Someone comes," Valdez said to Amador.

"We are ready for whoever it may be," Amador said calmly. "We have plenty of guns, and we can easily kill however many might be coming if they mean us harm— as easily as we can kill those three against the wall."

Time seemed to stop. Amador and Valdez stood stiffly, their eyes fixed on the entrance to the valley. The men, gathered in a group not far away, all had their hands on their guns.

Jessie wanted to run, but she knew she wouldn't get far before being gunned down. She held her ground and waited.

A rider entered the valley, a cloud of dust rising behind him and then enveloping him as he rode toward the hacienda with the wind at his back. It was not until he was within a few yards of them all that Jessie recognized the horseman as Diego Ruiz.

"Who are you?" Valdez yelled at the young man as Diego drew rein and stared at Jessie and Ki standing against the wall.

"My man, he asks you a question," Amador snapped. "Answer it, boy."

The last word Amador had spoken seemed to catch Diego's attention. "I am not a boy. I am a man. My name, it is Diego Ruiz. I have come to join you, Colonel Amador. You and your brave men."

Amador and Valdez exchanged amused glances. "What need have we of you?" Amador asked.

Diego continued to sit his saddle, an expression of dogged determination on his face.

"How will we chase this would-be bandit away from here, Valdez?" Amador inquired mockingly. "He is too skinny and, I think, too chickenhearted to be one of us."

"I can be of use to you, Colonel," Diego declared firmly. "I can shoot. I can steal. I can follow orders. I will soon become your right-hand man, you will see. Just give me a chance to prove myself to you."

Amador grinned. "You say you want to prove yourself to me, do you?"

Diego nodded eagerly.

"Step down then."

Diego got out of the saddle. When he was standing in front of Amador, the colonel said, "You say you can shoot?"

"Yes, sir, I can shoot good."

"But you have no gun."

Diego blushed. "I have no money to buy a gun, Colonel."

"But you can shoot one if you had one to shoot, you say. That is so, yes?"

Another eager nod from Diego.

"Then take this gun." Amador pulled Jessie's revolver from his waistband and handed it to Diego. "Now you have a gun. Now you can be a bad boy. Forgive me, Diego Ruiz, I mean a bad *man*." Diego stared transfixed at the gun in his hand. "Valdez," Amador said, "what shall we have Diego Ruiz shoot for us today?"

Valdez hesitated a moment and then, guessing what the colonel had in mind, said, "Them," and pointed to the three people lined up against the wall.

"Ah, a splendid idea, Valdez, a simply splendid idea." Amador turned to Diego. "Those three people standing against the wall over there—you will shoot them for me."

Diego's gaze shifted to Jessie, to Ki, to Dominguez. "But . . . why?"

"You have told me," Amador said in a chilly voice, "that you can steal and follow orders. You lied to me! You do not follow the very first order I, your colonel, give to you. Go away from here. You will not be one of us."

Diego stiffened as if Amador had just struck him. His eyes blazed as he gripped the butt of Jessie's revolver in both hands and turned. Taking aim at Dominguez, he began to squeeze the trigger, shutting his eyes as he did so.

"Stop!" Amador shouted.

Diego's eyes snapped open.

"You cannot shoot what you cannot see, *muchacho*. Do you shut your eyes because you are afraid to see the faces of those you would shoot? That is the way of a woman. Are you a woman?"

Diego furiously shook his head. He planted his feet, so that his legs formed an inverted V, and took aim again at Dominguez. He swallowed hard several times, his Adam's apple bobbing. His upper teeth appeared and got a firm grip on his lower lip.

"*Fuego!*" Valdez shouted.

But Diego did not fire as he had just been ordered to do. His arms slowly lowered until the gun in his hands pointed at the ground. He hung his head, blinking back tears.

Amador, spitting a string of obscenities at Diego, took the gun from him and returned it to his waistband. "*Go!*"

Diego flinched under the lash of Amador's order. He climbed back into the saddle, turned his horse and galloped away, leaving Amador's mocking laughter behind him.

When Diego had disappeared through the pass leading from the valley, the colonel, his laughter fading away, said, "Shoot him," to Valdez and pointed to Dominguez.

As Valdez took aim at the trembling man, Dominguez uttered a terrified cry and began to run.

For several seconds, the only sound was that made by his boots striking the hardpan beneath them. Then there was another sound—the loud report of Valdez's gun.

Dominguez, hit high in the back, threw up his arms, threw back his head, faltered in his flight and fell forward to lie facedown and unmoving in the dirt.

Jessie gritted her teeth and stared in horrified fascination at the body of Dominguez where it lay like a thrown-away doll in the early morning but already broiling sun. She forced herself to look away, and as she did her eyes fell on her gun in Amador's waistband.

"Good shot!" Amador said and clapped Valdez companionably on the shoulder. "One down, two to go."

As he turned his gaze on Jessie, she raised her eyes and smiled in what she hoped was a seductive manner, although she was feeling nothing remotely erotic, only a clawing fear that was making her stomach lurch.

Amador's eyes flickered as he continued to stare at her.

Her smile broadened and her tongue slid out to lick her lips as his earlier words spoken to Valdez, some of them, echoed in her mind:

"I would like to have the woman. I would like very much to have her."

"Colonel," she said in a throaty voice, "come here." She was aware of the sidelong look Ki had just given her, but she did not acknowledge it. She beckoned to Amador.

He put out a hand and forced Valdez to lower his gun, which had been aimed at Ki. He took a tentative step toward Jessie, a puzzled expression on his face, and then, when she beckoned to him again, he took quick strides in her direction, a man obviously in a hurry.

"You have something to say to me?" he asked when he reached her.

"I want to make a bargain with you."

"You who are about to die—what have you to bargain with, my pretty one?"

Jessie's hands rose and cupped her breasts. She let one hand slide down her body to clutch her crotch. Her eyes bored into Amador's, but she did not speak.

She did not have to. Amador moaned, his eyes moving from the hand on her breast to the one between her legs. "What do you want?" he asked huskily.

"I want you to spare Ki's life."

"In exchange for which you will—" Amador began, but Jessie interrupted him.

"Yes, I will."

Amador's breath gusted out of his mouth as he moaned like a man approaching a sexual climax.

"Jessie, no."

She heard Ki's words, but she paid him no attention as she reached out and linked her arm in Amador's.

"Jessie—"

Whatever Ki had been about to say was drowned out by the colonel's shouted command, "Valdez, don't shoot this man. He is to live."

"But, Colonel—"

"Silence!" Amador bellowed in the voice of a bull. "You will do as I say." He disengaged himself from Jessie and went over to where an obviously disappointed Valdez was standing. The two men spoke briefly together in hushed tones, and then Amador, grinning, returned to Jessie and offered her his arm.

She took it and they made their way into the hacienda.

In the courtyard, Amador halted and embraced Jessie, his great arms drawing her toward him, but the bulk of his belly, which overhung his belt, kept her at a distance from his eager lips. The kiss he was trying to deliver was not consummated, as Jessie drew away from him, smiled and said, as she shook a finger at him, "Not so fast. We have time. Lots of time. All the time in the world. We have today— and tonight."

"Come." He took her hand and practically dragged her across the courtyard, up the stairs and into his bedroom.

They had no sooner entered the room than Jessie, steeling herself, placed her hands on either side of Amador's face,

155

leaned over and kissed him with feigned passion.

"*Ahhh,*" he sighed as Jessie began to unbutton his shirt.

As she ran her fingers through the mat of curly hair that covered his chest, he sighed again and reached for her.

She reached for her gun, which was in his waistband.

"What—" He never got to finish his question.

"*Callate la boca!*" Jessie snapped, stepping back.

Amador, his eyes on the black bore of the gun in her hand, obeyed her order to shut up.

Before he had time to gather his wits about him following this unexpected development, Jessie raised her gun and slammed its barrel down upon the crown of his head.

No sound escaped Amador's lips as he crumpled like a dropped sack of grain and fell to the floor.

Jessie turned and ran. Out of the bedroom. Down the hall and then the steps. Into the courtyard and outside, where she called out, "Ki!"

He was still standing with his back to the wall, which was the first thing that surprised her. The second thing was the way Valdez was continuing to aim his gun at Ki despite Amador's earlier order to his underling to let Ki live.

"You're fast in more ways than one!" Valdez called, turning toward Jessie. "Drop your gun!"

"Drop *your* gun!" Jessie countered, not relishing one bit the Mexican standoff she found herself in with Valdez.

He merely laughed at her order instead of obeying it. "You can shoot me if you want to. But, if you do, your friend, Ki, goes down with me. I'll drop him at the same time you drop me. Fair trade?"

Jessie knew that Valdez knew she wouldn't consider his proposal anything like a fair trade. She wanted more than anything else at that moment to shoot Valdez, but the one thing she wanted least at that same moment was to see Ki get shot. One desire effectively canceled out the other. She had no real choice. She dropped her gun.

"Smart move, señorita," Valdez declared triumphantly.

"Kick your gun over this way."

Jessie did so, and he picked it up. He screamed then as the *shuriken* that had appeared in Ki's hand suddenly hurtled through the air and bit into his right wrist, causing him to drop his revolver.

Jessie, wasting no time, picked up her gun as well as Valdez's.

"Stop them!" shouted Colonel Amador as he appeared in an open window on the second floor of the hacienda.

Valdez went after Jessie and Ki as they sprinted toward the spot where their horses still stood in front of the hacienda, where they had left them upon their arrival at the gang's headquarters.

"Keep going!" Ki yelled to Jessie and then spun around and went for the pursuing Valdez.

The Mexican, seeing Ki coming, slowed his pace and seemed about to turn and flee. But instead he halted and stood his ground, waiting for Ki, his uninjured left hand outstretched and ready to grab, ready to strangle . . .

Ki, in a swift blur of graceful movement, lowered his left shoulder, bent his left leg, rolled forward and down until his shoulder hit the ground, brought his right foot up and rammed it deep into Valdez's solar plexus. Ki was instantly up on his feet again and racing back to join Jessie, who was aboard her bay and holding the reins of his horse for him.

Behind him, Valdez was doubled over and gasping desperately for air. Blood from his right wrist, which Ki's throwing star had savaged, stained his clothes.

Ki vaulted into the saddle and together with Jessie went galloping away from the hacienda toward the canyon leading out of the valley.

Amador's frantic, almost crazed, words followed them: "Catch them! Stop them, somebody! Am I destined to spend my life with fools who can do nothing right? *Kill them!*"

"Jessie," Ki called out over the sound of their horses' pounding hooves, "I wish you hadn't—"

"I didn't." She gave him a grin as her coppery hair flew out behind her in the wind.

"You mean your offer to Amador was a ploy?"

She nodded. "Before I left him I put him to sleep. With this." She tapped the butt of the .38 she had reholstered.

"Ironic," Ki remarked, smiling to himself.

"What's ironic?"

"Just now, back there, Amador was accusing his men of being fools he had to suffer. I think that's a clear-cut case of the pot calling the kettle black. I mean, he fell for your ploy. That makes him, in my book, a first-class fool."

"Don't be too hard on him. Most men have, at one time or another in their lives, played the fool for some woman."

Ki silently admitted to himself that Jessie was right. His own experiences with various and sundry women down through the years proved her so.

"There's something I don't understand, Ki."

"What is it?"

"When I came out of the hacienda, it looked to me like Valdez was about to shoot you."

"He was."

"But Colonel Amador ordered him not to. I heard him say so. Valdez was to let you live."

"Do you remember that Amador and Valdez had a brief conversation before you and he went inside?"

"Yes, I remember."

"After you and the Colonel had gone, Valdez told me that Amador had just told him that he was to kill me despite the bargain he struck with you—your favors for my life. Valdez told me he was waiting only for you or Amador to reappear. When either one of you came out of the hacienda, he said he had been told that would be his signal that the deal between you and Amador had been consummated to the colonel's satisfaction and thus Valdez would be at liberty to eliminate me."

"That Amador is a scoundrel, no two ways about it."

"Valdez also told me that Amador intended to let Valdez kill you as well—again, after the colonel had had his way with you."

"I suppose I shouldn't be too hard on Amador, should I?"

"What do you mean?"

"Well, I had no intention of keeping my end of our little bargain, and I didn't keep it. So how can I blame him for plotting to renege on his part of that same bargain—namely, to let you live."

Ki, suddenly uneasy, glanced over his shoulder.

"What's the matter?" Jessie asked him.

"I think I heard something. I think they're coming after us."

"I didn't hear anything."

"Listen."

Jessie did, trying to hear any sounds other than those made by their creaking saddle leathers and their horses' hooves, she heard it then, the sound of other horses on the trail behind them.

"Ki, you've got the keenest ears this side of the Mississippi," she said. "I swear you could hear an ant crossing a rock."

"We'd better make tracks, Jessie, and make them fast. I've next to no doubt that the riders behind us are from the hacienda."

They dug their heels into their horses, and the bay and the black responded with bursts of speed that sent their manes flying. Just before they entered a grove of cottonwoods growing along the bank of a broad stream, Jessie looked back over her shoulder and saw Colonel Amador far behind them at the head of a group of his men, Valdez among them.

Neither she nor Ki spoke as they drove their horses hard. They weaved through the trees, ducking low-hanging branches and jumping over deadfalls, as they followed the curving course of the stream.

"There's somebody up ahead of us," Ki shouted to make himself heard above the noise of their horses' pounding hooves.

As they came closer to the lone man in the distance, they recognized Diego Ruiz, who was slowly riding along the bank of the stream.

He turned at the sound of their approach and then drew rein to wait for them to join him. When they had done so, he asked, "How did you escape from the Colonel?"

"There's no time to go into that now," Ki answered. "Amador and his boys are trailing us."

"I will help you fight them," Diego volunteered.

"With what?" Ki asked. "Your bare hands?"

"You both have guns," Diego noted. "That will count for something."

"So does that bunch behind us," Ki pointed out. "We've got to make a stand even though they've got us outgunned."

"We could continue making a run for it," Jessie suggested.

"I don't know about your bay, but my black is about ready to give out on me. I vote for making a stand and trying to run them off. Maybe if we can kill a couple of them—maybe even Amador himself—the rest will turn tail and—"

"They come!" Diego cried, pointing at the riders rounding a bend behind them.

"It's them all right," Ki muttered.

"Follow me!" Diego commanded. Without waiting for a response from either Ki or Jessie, he flogged his horse with his reins and went galloping west.

After exchanging puzzled glances, Jessie and Ki rode out after him. Five minutes later, after crossing the stream, Diego led them to what looked like a sheer wall of rock rising out of the tableland to form a sky-high mesa.

He sprang from the saddle and led his horse toward the solid-seeming wall. He turned and grinned at Jessie and Ki

160

as he held aside some thick brush that was growing at the base of the cliff. His action revealed the entrance to a cave that had been hidden by the vegetation. He led his horse through the opening, as Jessie and Ki did theirs.

"This place, it is only a mile from Del Rio," he told them when they were all inside the cave. "We can hide here until the colonel tires of searching for us."

"I'm glad we met you," Jessie said. "If we hadn't, we never would have known about this cave."

Diego hung his head. In a low voice, a voice that was little more than a murmur, he said, "I am not glad you met me." He looked up then and, in a stronger voice, added, "I mean I am glad I met you and was able to bring you here but . . . " His voice trailed away.

"I think I know what you mean," Jessie said. "You wish Ki and I hadn't seen what happened to you at the hacienda."

"*Si*. I am ashamed of what happened to me there."

"There's no need to be," Ki said. "You couldn't kill a man in cold blood. I don't see that that's something to be ashamed of. On the contrary, I think that's something to be proud of. The fact that you couldn't kill Dominguez back there shows me that you're a decent man."

"But I wanted to be a bandit," Diego said plaintively.

"You wanted to have enough money to buy the things you need," Jessie said. "For yourself and for Marisol. That is not the same as wanting to be a bandit."

Diego stared at her in silence for a moment. Then he began to smile. "I never thought of it that way. But, *si,* what you have said, it is true. It is money that made me want to go to Colonel Amador and ask him to let me ride with him. My sister needs many things. A dress that is not worn out with many washings. More food than we have, so that she is not always at least a little bit hungry. I sometimes wish I could buy her an amber comb to wear in her hair. I know she does not really *need* such a thing. And yet . . .

161

and yet sometimes I think people need more than just food and a roof over their heads. Sometimes I think they need things that some would say they could live without. It is hard for me to put it in the English. It is like a man who has a dream. He wants to make a good life for his wife and children. He does not really need his dream. And yet it comforts him and gives him a taste of happiness when the nights are long or when the thunder shakes the sky."

"You're right," Jessie said. "People do need their dreams. Without them, they are little more than beasts."

Diego's eyes glowed. "Then you do understand."

"We understand," Ki assured him.

"If I had much money," Diego said dreamily, "I would go to a big city like Matamoras, and there I would hire someone to come to Del Rio to teach our children how to write their names and how to read the words in books, so that they could become wise and be more than ever they thought they could be, any of them, boys and girls both, when they grow up.

"I would give money to Padre Juan. His order, they do not send him much money from Spain. They are poor, so he is poor also. The church, it needs work. Padre Juan speaks sometimes of selling the *santos*—the gold statue of the crucified Christ that hangs in our church to get the money he needs. That would be like selling his heart. I know. He will not say so, but the idea of selling the *santos,* it hurts him. But what else is he to do?

"*Si,* if money would come to Del Rio, it would find many things to do there. It would find many hearts to make happy with the things it could buy. A teacher for the children. A new floor and many candles for the church. Goats and chickens to give us milk and eggs. Maybe a cow. Maybe *two* cows!"

Diego went to the brush that covered the cave's entrance and cautiously peered through it, the sunlight leaking through the branches and dappling his face.

162

"Can you see anything?" Jessie asked him.

"There is no sign of the colonel and his men. They are busy chasing the wild goose as you Americanos say. Better they try to catch it than us, *sí?*"

"Yes," Ki said, "much better."

Diego turned toward him and Jessie. "I have the idea. You have guns. The village of Del Rio has many men like me. Men and guns together could fight Colonel Amador. Maybe drive him away from here so that we may live in peace. That reminds me. Jessie, did you get your brooch back from the colonel? The brooch you told Padre Juan the Americano who was in Del Rio stole from you?" Jessie shook her head. "Amador still has it? Then you have something to gain in a fight against the colonel. Your brooch. We men of Del Rio, we have our honor and the safety of our families to gain. It would be a good fight, do you not think so? A fight with much for all of us to gain if, God willing, we win it."

Jessie glanced at Ki, who said, "Your idea may not be a bad one, Diego."

"It is not a bad one, señor. It is a good one. The best one I have ever had. Let us go now to the village—it is not far from here—and get ready to make for ourselves a plan to do battle with Colonel Amador."

Jessie went to the cave's entrance and peered through the brush covering it. "It looks like the coast's clear." She led her bay out of the cave then with Ki and Diego, leading their horses, following her.

Moments later, the three of them were riding hard toward their destination—the village of Del Rio.

163

Chapter 10

The village of Del Rio was quiet as Jessie, Ki and Diego rode into it. There were few people moving about, and those who were did so quickly, as if they were in a hurry to get out of the sun. A dead dog lay near the steps of the church, blood on its fur.

Jessie didn't like it. The quiet—there was too much of it. When Diego touched the brim of his sombrero to a woman carrying a basket full of herbs and said, "*Buenos dias*, Señora Gonzalez," the woman did not look at him or answer but hurried away into the dark doorway of a house.

"They think I am one of the colonel's men now," Diego said. "That must be why Senōra Gonzalez turned away from me like I carried the plague. All of Del Rio must know by now that I went away to join Colonel Amador. I made no secret of my plan. Probably Padre Juan prayed for me at mass this morning."

"Father Juan sounds as if he's praying pretty hard right now," Ki commented as the priest's raised voice could be heard coming from the church. Beneath it was the lower but not softer sound of another man's voice.

"He will not like what we will do," Diego declared, shaking his head. "A man of peace is the padre. He will not like

164

it that we men of the village of Del Rio are going to fight with you against Colonel Amador and his bandits. He will say we should turn the other cheek. He will tell us to love our enemies." Diego spat upon the ground. "I will not turn my other cheek to Colonel Amador, and I hate my enemies, who are also the enemies of my village."

"Where are all the men?" Jessie asked, looking about the seemingly deserted village.

A woman appeared at a window in one of the adobe buildings and closed its shutters.

"There are fields over that way," Diego said. "The men of the village work the fields. You stay here. I will go and tell them to come to the plaza, where we will make plans for the war we will wage against the bandits."

Diego rode away, leaving Jessie and Ki alone in the empty plaza.

The voices they had heard coming from the church were silent now. The village itself was silent. No baby cried; no dog barked.

When Marisol Ruiz suddenly appeared on the far side of the plaza and saw Jessie and Ki, she halted abruptly and stood there staring at them as if she were seeing ghosts—or demons. There was an unreadable expression on her face.

Jessie raised a hand in greeting. Her gesture seemed to frightened Marisol, who turned and started back the way she had come. Then she stopped, turned back and made an almost violent gesture with both of her hands.

"It looks," Ki said, "as if she's telling us to go away."

"Maybe she thinks we're here on behalf of Colonel Amador. There are no secrets in a small village like this. Father Juan probably let it be known that we intended to join the colonel's gang."

"Marisol!" Diego called out as he rode into the plaza and waved to his sister.

She didn't acknowledge his greeting.

He beckoned to her as he dismounted.

She didn't move for a moment and then, taking slow, small steps, she started in his direction. It seemed to take her a long time to reach her brother, and when she did she did not speak but threw her arms around him and hugged him to her, her face buried against his chest.

"What is this, my sister?" he asked, holding her out at arm's length in front of him. "What is it makes you cry? You are not happy to see me?"

"I am happy to see you, Diego."

"Then why do you weep?" When Marisol stayed silent, Diego asked, "Where are the men of the village? They do not work the fields. It is not the hour of the *siesta*—"

Diego fell silent as a solemn-visaged Father Juan emerged from the interior of his church and stood on the top of the steps with his arms at his sides, gazing at the four people in the plaza.

"You have come home, my son," he said at last, addressing Diego.

"*Sí*, Padre."

"You have returned to Del Rio as well," he said then to Jessie and Ki.

"We have, Father," Jessie said. "We were wondering why the village is so quiet. Why are there no people about?"

"They stay inside. The sun, it is very hot."

"What happened to the dog, Father?" Ki asked.

The priest stared down at the dead dog in the plaza. "An unfortunate incident," he said softly. "Would you like to come inside the church? It is a bit cooler there."

When Diego began to climb the steps of the church but Ki and Jessie remained where they were, Father Juan said, "Come inside and tell me what happened to the three of you at the hacienda of Colonel Amador."

Jessie and Ki began to mount the steps. When they reached the spot where the priest stood waiting for them, he held up a hand.

"Your gun," he said to Jessie. "It does not belong in the

house of the Lord. Leave it on the doorstep. No one will steal it."

Jessie was about to unholster her gun when Ki put a hand on her forearm, preventing her from doing so.

"You didn't ask Jessie to leave her gun outside the last time we visited your church," Ki said. "Why now, Father?"

For a moment, the priest seemed flustered. Then, smiling, he said, "Ah, I grow old. Sometimes I forget things. When you were here before I forgot to ask you to leave your gun outside, Jessie."

Ki did not remove his hand from Jessie's forearm. "Another thing, Father. You didn't answer my question about that dog lying down there in the dirt. You called it an 'unfortunate incident.' How did the dog die?"

Instead of answering, Father Juan turned and hurried into his church.

"There's something funny going on here, if you ask me," Ki said. "And I think Father Juan knows what it is."

"Let's go talk to him." Jessie withdrew her arm from Ki's grasp and hurried into the church before he could stop her.

He reluctantly followed her, and Diego and Marisol followed him. As they entered the church, Ki stiffened at the sight of Jessie standing with her hands in the air as two men who he recognized as members of Colonel Amador's gang of bandits flanked her. One of them took her gun from its holster and thrust it into his waistband.

The other man leveled the revolver in his hand in the direction of Ki and his two companions.

"I am sorry for this, Jessie," Father Juan said as he stood to one side, his hands folded as if in prayer.

"Inside," one of Amador's men barked in Spanish. "All of you."

Ki stared past the guns to where a number of men from the village were seated in the church's pews.

"Why are these gunmen here?" Jessie asked Father Juan.

Before he could answer her, from behind stout pillars and pedestaled statues of saints, other members of Amador's gang stepped out, all of them with guns in their hands and grim expressions on their faces.

Colonel Amador himself emerged from the dark confines of the confessional booth.

"What's going on here?" Ki shot at him.

"Tell him, Juan," Amador said to the priest, beside whom Diego and Marisol were standing.

"They came here in search of you," the priest explained to Jessie and Ki. "Victoriano told me he had seen you meet young Diego outside the village and then the three of you disappeared and none of his men could find you. He told me he believed you would come here to Del Rio sooner or later. Or if you two didn't, he knew that Diego would, and, once he did, he would be able to say where you had gone."

"Every man in the village must be here," Ki observed. "Why, Father?"

"Victoriano had his men round them up and bring them here to force me to do his bidding and to guarantee that no one in the village would reveal the presence of Victoriano and his men. He said if I failed to persuade you to enter the church unarmed where his men could take you prisoner, he would shoot the villagers."

"You are a suspicious man, Ki," Amador said almost jovially. "We heard you asking the good priest questions about such things as the dead dog outside. You wanted to know why the dog died, I believe. Well, I will tell you. It died because I shot it to show the good priest what I would do to the men inside the church if he refused to do what I ordered him to do."

"I am sorry," Father Juan again told Jessie and Ki. "I was afraid for the lives of my parishioners. Please try to understand."

Neither Ki nor Jessie said anything.

168

"Victoriano told me he only wants you to give him back the ruby brooch you took from him, Jessie," the priest added sorrowfully. "If you do that, he promised me that neither you nor Ki would be harmed."

Jessie stared at Father Juan and slowly shook her head.

"You will not do it? You will not give him the brooch?" The priest's eyes were sad. "Think, Jessie. It is only a piece of jewelry. Surely you would not insist upon keeping it when these men"—he indicated the men in the church's pews, who were watching and listening to him with tense fascination—"will be killed if you do not surrender the brooch."

"Father, I do not have it."

"But—" The priest glanced at Amador. "Victoriano told me you stole it from him. He said he would let all the men he took prisoner go if I brought you to him and you surrendered the brooch. I do not understand."

"This situation is easy to understand, Father," Ki said. "The simple fact is the colonel lied to you about Jessie having the brooch."

"I did try to get it back," Jessie added. "I had it in my hand, but he caught me in the act of taking it and took it away from me. He was going to kill Ki and me, and he would have if we had not managed to escape from him."

"*Exactamente!*" Colonel Amador crowed. "I have played you for the fool that you are, Juan."

"What are you going to do with them?" Father Juan asked Amador, indicating Ki and Jessie.

"What am I going to do with them?" Amador repeated, his gaze shifting from Ki to Jessie. "Why, I am going to kill them, that is what I am going to do with them, because they tried to make a fool out of *me*, Colonel Victoriano Amador!"

"No," protested the priest but in a voice made weak by shock. "Thou shalt not kill, Victoriano."

"I would not have survived as a child in the city streets if

I had not killed, Juan," the Colonel snarled. "You would not have survived either, in those days when we were children, if you had not learned to break the commandments—to lie, to cheat, to steal food to put in your miserable belly. So do not speak to me of the way your God says we should live. I have no use for Him—"

Amador suddenly fell silent in midsentence. A smile spread over his face as he turned his head toward the altar. "I lie, Juan. I do have use for your God. At least, I have use for His image, which hangs there above your altar."

"What are you saying?" Father Juan asked, following Amador's gaze.

"I am saying that I will take that golden statue of your crucified God, and I will sell Him in Mexico City for much money to a dealer in gold who will melt Him down and turn Him into ingots."

An ominous murmur ran through the crowd of men in the pews at the colonel's announcement. It was followed by one man among them rising to his feet and saying one word: "No."

Valdez took aim at the man, who promptly resumed his seat.

"You have taken all we have to give," Father Juan said to his boyhood friend and former protector. "Do not take this last precious thing. It is not the gold that matters. It is a sacrilege to desecrate the *santos*. Beware, Victoriano. Pay heed to the welfare of your immortal soul. God is not mocked."

"There is another thing we will take as well, Juan," Amador said. He pointed at Marisol, who stood half-hidden behind her brother. "*All* of us will take her," he added.

This time it was Diego's turn to say, "No."

Amador turned to him. "You would deny us a taste of your sweet sister, Ruiz?"

Diego, stepping in front of Marisol to shield her, said,

170

"I will defy you. I will die if I must to defend her."

"There is plenty of death here for all of you," Amador said quietly. "We will not neglect to give you your share, *impudente*."

"You call me 'bold one,' " Diego said. "I will show you that you speak the truth." He lunged at Amador.

Valdez, stepping to his leader's side and raising his gun, struck Diego with it, sending him sprawling to the floor.

Marisol, seeing her brother fall, ran to him, but before she could kneel beside him, Valdez seized her wrist and pulled her toward him. Holding her with one hand, his other hand gripping his gun, he shouted, "You, Toro, and you, Francisco—take down the *santos*."

As the two men Valdez had designated moved toward the altar, the men in the pews rose as one man and blocked their path. Toro and Francisco leveled their guns at the crowd and ordered them to step aside. As the men reluctantly did so, Toro and Francisco moved closer to the altar. But long before they reached it, the unarmed villagers made their move. Picking up the pews in which they had been sitting while being held captive, they used them as battering rams against Toro and Francisco.

Both men fired their weapons, but their shots went wild as first one and then a second pew plowed into them, breaking their bones and, in the case of Toro, also knocking several of his teeth out of his mouth.

The colonel shouted a series of orders in fiery Spanish, and his men responded to them. Shots were fired at the villagers, who continued to use the church pews to batter any of Amador's men they could reach. The volley of gunfire momentarily subdued them; they crouched down out of the line of fire, holding the wooden pews in front of them to ward off the additional rounds Amador's men were firing at them.

In the noise and gun smoke, Ki turned and ran from the church. When he returned, he had his rifle in his hand. He

171

took aim at Valdez and fired but missed his man, as Marisol cowered in a corner behind a painted plaster statue of the Virgin.

Valdez ran behind a pillar and from that vantage point fired two rounds, which entered the backs of two of the villagers who had taken refuge behind what was now a tall pile of pews in the middle of the floor. The men Valdez had hit lurched upward and then spun around, one to the right, one to the left, and fell over their makeshift barricade, staining it with their blood.

Jessie, her eyes on the man who had disarmed her and who was firing steadily at the villagers behind their barricade, made her way around a pillar and then between statues of Saint Anthony holding the Infanta and Saint Francis with a bird on his shoulder and a deer standing by his side. When she was directly behind her quarry, she made ready to attack him.

But before she could do so, two of the villagers rose up and hurled wrought iron prie-dieus at their attackers. One of them struck the man Jessie had been stalking. He fell backward, his gun going off as he shouted curses in colorful Spanish. She ran forward and jerked her .38 out of his waistband. As she did so, he saw her. His lips twisted in a snarl as he rolled to one side and took aim at her . . .

Her first shot blew his brains out.

Amador was still shouting orders, and his men, those who had not been wounded like Toro and Francisco and others who had also taken crippling blows in various parts of their bodies from the pews and prie-dieus, tried their best to obey them. Then Amador disappeared in the shifting smoke and battling bodies.

Minutes later, it was Father Juan who spotted his once-upon-a-time friend. The colonel had vaulted the sanctuary railing and was heading for the altar.

"No!" the priest screamed, but his one word could not be heard above the melee. He ran toward the altar, intent

172

on stopping Amador from stealing the golden *santos*.

But he was forced to halt when two of his parishioners unwittingly blocked his path as they lifted the brazen stand, which was stained with wax from the many lighted votive candles it held. As Father Juan stood there unable to move forward, the two men raised the stand above their heads. They hurled it at a cluster of three of Amador's men, who were each down on one knee as they fired into the group of villagers that had become an enraged mob as they defended their church and themselves from the marauders who had invaded their village one more dreadful time.

Two of the three men screamed as the brazen stand and its blazing candles flew toward them. All three screamed when it struck them broadside and the candles spilling from it spattered hot wax on their bare skins and the candles' flames set their clothes and hair afire. They rose up together and, dropping their guns and raising their arms that had begun to burn like torches, they ran for the door of the church. One made it. The other two fell flaming to the stone floor, where they rolled over and over, screaming as they did so, their burning flesh giving off a sickening sweet odor for a brief time before it charred and cracked open to reveal bones and the men died.

Outside the church, the third man who had fled from the church threw himself into the fountain in the middle of the plaza. Steam rose from him. Writhing and still steaming, he died there.

Diego sprinted forward, shoving men out of his way, seemingly heedless of the danger he was in. He, too, vaulted the altar railing and entered the sanctuary, as Colonel Amador had done only moments before. At the altar, he reached for Amador, who was standing on it, unmindful of the monstrance he had overturned and which had fallen to the floor, the Host still within it. His hands landed on Amador. He seized the man's belt and jerked backward.

Amador tried to kick Diego but missed. He gripped the

173

representation of the crucified Christ and held tightly to it to maintain his balance.

Diego pulled harder, cursing the colonel at the top of his voice for attempting to steal the golden *santos*, damning him over and over again with wild and angry words.

Amador continued to cling to the *santos*.

Diego continued to pull on his belt.

A moment later, Amador fell from the altar, landing on top of Diego.

The heavy six-foot-long *santos*, torn from the wall, landed on top of Amador.

Diego managed to struggle out from under the crushing weight of both the human and the golden bodies. He got shakily to his feet and stood there panting, unmindful of the noise and the acrid stench of gunpowder that filled the church.

He was still staring down at Amador when Father Juan arrived at his side.

"Victoriano?" the priest breathed. And then he saw what had happened. He saw the golden spike that was a part of the crucified Christ's crown of thorns—the golden spike which had pierced Amador's left eye and then entered his skull to impale his brain.

"*In nomine patris, et filii, et spiritu sancto,*" Father Juan began, making the sign of the cross above the body of the dead Colonel Amador.

But his words were drowned out by a shout—more of a scream—that came from Valdez, a scream that was followed by "*Lo mataron!*"

They killed him!

Valdez's words galvanized the survivors among Amador's men, who, at the sight of their lifeless leader's body, had been standing paralyzed, as were the villagers. They sprang into action, all of them heading for Diego Ruiz and Father Juan, who had their backs to them, shrieking and angrily brandishing their weapons.

Jessie raised her own weapon and, holding it in both hands, took aim and fired several shots in quick succession.

Two of the colonel's men went down and did not rise.

But the others continued on their course of vengeance, heading straight for Diego and Father Juan, who were now standing motionless in the face of the advancing horde.

"Kill them!" Valdez shouted and fired a shot that narrowly missed the priest.

Ki took a *shuriken* from his pocket and threw it at Valdez. It hit him in the left side of his head, slicing off part of his ear. As blood spurted from the wound, Valdez fired at Ki.

Ki, anticipating the man's move, swiftly sidestepped out of the way of the oncoming round, and Jessie swung around to squeeze off a shot that brought Valdez down.

The advancing bandits stopped in their tracks, their eyes shifting from the dead body of Colonel Amador to the equally dead body of his second in command, Valdez. One of the men crossed himself.

Then, as if someone had given a signal, although no one had, the survivors among Amador's men turned and, their boots clacking harshly on the floor, fled from the church.

Ki and Jessie went to the door of the church, where they stood, Jessie with her smoking gun in her hand, Ki with another *shuriken* in his, and watched as Amador's men retrieved their horses, which had been hidden behind an adobe building on the far side of the plaza, and rode away, most of them alone.

They were still standing there when Father Juan and Diego joined them.

"It's all over," Ki said.

"Thanks be to God." Father Juan sighed. "I must give the sacrament of extreme unction to Victoriano. But before I do, my friends, please try to forgive me for placing your lives in such grave danger. I made a terrible mistake in believing Victoriano when he told me he would not harm you."

175

"Excuse me," Jessie said as Ki said, "There is nothing to forgive, Father."

Jessie made her way into the church. Stepping gingerly around the bodies of villagers and bandits alike that littered the stone floor of the church, she made her way to Amador's corpse, which lay at the foot of the altar. Without disturbing the golden *santos*, which still lay upon him in a deadly embrace, she searched his pockets. When she had finished doing so, she sat back on her heels and hung her head.

The Firebird was not in any of the colonel's pockets.

Finally she rose and left the church. When she rejoined the others outside, she found that Marisol was with them. The girl, she thought, looked dazed. She looked to Jessie as if she were about to flee at the slightest ominous sound or sight.

Ki gave Jessie a questioning glance.

She shook her head. "Amador doesn't have my brooch on him."

"Maybe it is at the de León hacienda," Father Juan suggested.

"He carried it with him before," Jessie said. "I found it in his vest pocket when I tried to recover it earlier. I doubt that he would leave it unguarded at the hacienda. Someone might steal it from him." She managed the ghost of a smile.

"I am sorry," Father Juan told her. "I know how much the brooch meant to you. I know you have risked your life to retrieve it."

"We'll go to the hacienda," Ki said. "We'll search it. There's a chance—maybe a slim one—that the brooch might be there."

"The bandits," Marisol said nervously. "*They* might be there."

"I don't think they will be," Ki said. "They scattered. Now that their top two men are dead, chances are they'll drift."

176

"But if they are there, any of them," Jessie said firmly, "we'll deal with them." She holstered her gun and then shook hands with Father Juan. "Good-bye, Father."

"*Vaya con Dios*, Jessie." The priest shook hands with Ki.

Then both Jessie and Ki shook hands with Diego. Both of them embraced the still-trembling Marisol before turning and going down the steps to where their horses waited.

As they approached the entrance to the canyon that led to the valley where the de León hacienda was located, Ki drew rein and said, "Wait here for me, Jessie."

"Where are you going?"

"I'm going up on top of that cliff to see whether or not they've left anybody manning the heliograph up there. If there is somebody up there, I'll put him out of commission so nobody will be waiting to welcome us at the hacienda when we get there."

Jessie, when Ki had gone, waited impatiently where she had, at Ki's sensible suggestion, taken cover in a thick stand of timber. She sat her saddle uneasily, her eyes shifting from right to left as she watched the trail leading to the canyon's entrance, and the entrance itself.

No one emerged from the canyon, nor did anyone approach the entrance to it. Jessie was considering going after Ki when he reappeared, his horse slipping and sliding as it made its way down the steep descent from the cliff above.

"Nobody's up there," he told Jessie as she rode out to meet him. "If there's anybody at the hacienda, they won't know we're on our way."

He drew his rifle from his saddle scabbard, and as he did so Jessie's gun cleared leather.

They rode into the canyon, neither of them speaking, and then paused for a moment when they reached the entrance to the valley. They saw no signs of life anywhere near the hacienda. The front door was closed. Cloth curtains fluttered at an open upstairs window. No smoke rose from the stone chimney on the side of the building.

They moved forward cautiously, almost stealthily, their eyes scanning the area. No one appeared. No one fired upon them. No voice was raised either in greeting or to order them to drop their guns. They dismounted and, leaving their horses ground-hitched, went inside the hacienda.

The house was still. Dust motes drifted in the sunlight streaming through the windows.

"I don't know where to begin looking," Jessie said.

"I'll take the downstairs," Ki volunteered. "You take the upstairs."

As he began his search for the Firebird, Jessie climbed the stairs to the second floor and began hers.

With every drawer she opened and every closet she searched, her sense of sadness grew. The Firebird eluded her. She had begun to feel not only sad but vaguely bitter. Images from the past few days flashed through her mind. She saw again, as she went searching from room to room, James Barton's blue-eyed smile, and she could almost feel his arms around her as they had been that night at the party when it all began—the night he stole the brooch from her. She could see Bud Lomax's foxy face and hear his raucous laughter as he barked orders to his outlaws. Polly Jessup died again in her memory. She could hear Polly's husband, Clarence Jessup, whining over his loss of the brooch, which did not and never had belonged to him. Last of all came the image of Colonel Victoriano Amador and the skin-crawling sensation of his lips on hers. She thought of the misfortune the Firebird had seemed to bring to all of them.

She shuddered and left the room she had been searching.

"Did you find it?" Ki asked her as she slowly descended the staircase.

"No," she answered, her voice dull. "I don't think I'll ever see it again."

178

Ki went to her and put an arm around her shoulders. "I know how you feel. It's a bitter pill to swallow, the loss of the Firebird."

"I shall miss it, Ki. I loved that brooch. Not just the brooch itself but what it represented. For me, it represented a kind of continuity with the past as it passed from woman to woman in the Starbuck family."

"Listen!"

Jessie heard it, too, then—the sound of a single horse approaching the hacienda. She went to the window, drawing her gun, which she had holstered during her search. Ki joined her there after picking up his rifle, which he had leaned against the wall near the front door.

"It's Marisol Ruiz," Jessie said. "What in the world is she doing here?"

They went outside to find out.

"Jessie," Marisol cried as Jessie and Ki emerged from the hacienda. "I was afraid I would not find you. I was afraid you and Ki might have gone away."

"You followed us here," Ki said, curious. "Why?"

Marisol slid out of the saddle and came up to them. "After you left Del Rio, I spoke to Father Juan. I told him I had to go to confession. He said he would hear my confession later. He had to bury the colonel and the others who had been killed in the church, he said.

"But I told him it was important that he hear my confession right away. Finally he agreed to do so. When he heard what I had to confess, he told me I must do penance. I must make right what I had done wrong."

"I'm afraid I don't follow you, Marisol," Jessie said.

"What I did—I did it to help my people—the people of Del Rio. I did not do it for myself, Jessie. That is the truth. I swear to you it is!"

"*What* did you do?" Ki asked.

But it was Jessie to whom Marisol directed her answer. "When I was hiding behind the statue of the Virgin in the

179

church I thought surely I was going to die. I thought someone would shoot me. I tried several times to run from the
church, but every time I did, the fighting would come close
to where I was hiding and I did not dare move. Even when
the fighting finally ended, I was still afraid to move.

"But then I thought of your brooch, which Diego had
told me about and which Colonel Amador had said you had
stolen from him. Later, when I learned that he still had it—
I wished it was mine.

"Then, when I was the only one left alive in the church—
you and everyone else had left the church—I went to where
the colonel was lying and I quickly went through his pockets. I am ashamed of myself for what I did—"

"You found my brooch in one of the colonel's pockets,"
Jessie said, her face beginning to glow.

Marisol nodded. "It was in his vest pocket. When I
heard someone—someone who turned out to be you—
coming back into the church, I ran back and hid again
behind the statue of the Virgin. When you had passed me
by, I went outside as quickly as I could. You did not see
or hear me leave the church. I had hidden your ruby brooch
in my blouse."

"Where is it now?" Ki asked.

Marisol reached into her blouse and withdrew the Firebird. As she held it out to Jessie, it sparkled in the sunlight.

Jessie took it from her and held it close to her own breast,
her eyes closed as she silently offered a prayer of thanks-
giving for the safe return of her treasure.

" . . . and I was going to sell it in Matamoras or maybe Mexico City," Marisol was saying. "With the money
it would bring I was going to make life better for all the
people of Del Rio. Our children would not cry because they
were hungry. Padre Juan would not have to sell the *santos*—
the one Colonel Amador tried to steal from us today. Often
our padre says he must sell it to get the money to make our

180

lives a little bit better. But the people of the village would not let him do it.

"When you and Ki rode away to come here in search of the brooch, I felt great guilt. I knew I had done wrong. I wanted to confess my wrongdoing to Padre Juan. He it was who told me I must return the brooch to you. I know he was right to tell me to do that. I am sorry for what I did, Jessie."

Jessie stepped forward and took Marisol in her arms. "I understand why you did what you did. Your brother, Diego, he, too, told me of the dreams he had for the people of Del Rio. I have just now decided to put my brooch to good use. I will help you and Diego and all your friends and neighbors make those dreams come true."

Jessie stepped back, and as Marisol gazed at her, a question in her eyes, Jessie looked down at the Firebird in her hand for a long silent moment and then slowly extended her hand toward Marisol.

The young woman looked down at the brooch and then up at Jessie.

"Take it, Marisol. Sell it. Buy what you and the others in your village so desperately need. It will do more good that way than it ever could in my jewel box at home."

"Jessie—" Marisol tried to speak but could say no more. Tears filled her eyes.

"You'd better get back home," Jessie told her gently. "You'll be wanting to tell the others in Del Rio of the good fortune that has befallen them."

"Oh, yes!" Marisol cried and quickly boarded her horse. She waved with the hand that held the Firebird. It flashed its own bright red farewell to Jessie. Then Marisol called out, "May the good God keep you both."

Jessie and Ki watched her ride away, and then they, too, boarded their horses and began their long journey home.

A special offer for people who enjoy reading the best Westerns published today. If you enjoyed this book, subscribe now and get . . .

TWO FREE

A $5.90 VALUE—NO OBLIGATION

If you enjoyed this book and would like to read more of the very best Westerns being published today, you'll want to subscribe to True Value's Western Home Subscription Service. If you enjoyed the book you just read and want more of the most exciting, adventurous, action packed Westerns, subscribe now.

Each month the editors of True Value will select the 6 very best Westerns from America's leading publishers for special readers like you. You'll be able to preview these new titles as soon as they are published, FREE for ten days with no obligation.

TWO FREE BOOKS

When you subscribe, we'll send you your first month's shipment of the newest and best 6 Westerns for you to preview. With your first shipment, two of these books will be yours as our introductory gift to you absolutely FREE, regardless of what you decide to do. If you like them, as much as we think you will, keep all six books but pay for just 4 at the low subscriber rate of just $2.45 each. If you decide to return them, keep 2 of the titles as our gift. No obligation.

Special Subscriber Savings

When you become a True Value subscriber you'll save money several ways. First, all regular monthly selections will be billed at the low subscriber price of just $2.45 each. That's

WESTERNS!

at least a savings of $3.00 each month below the publishers price. Second, there is never any shipping, handling or other hidden charges—Free home delivery. What's more there is no minimum number of books you must buy, you may return any selection for full credit and you can cancel your subscription at any time. A TRUE VALUE!

Mail the coupon below

To start your subscription and receive 2 FREE WESTERNS, fill out the coupon below and mail it today. We'll send your first shipment which includes 2 FREE BOOKS as soon as we receive it.